CELADON SUMMER

CELADON SUMMER

•

JO MOREHOUSE

AVALON BOOKS
THOMAS BOUREGY AND COMPANY, INC.
401 LAFAYETTE STREET
NEW YORK, NEW YORK 10003

© Copyright 1996 by Jo Morehouse
Library of Congress Catalog Card Number: 96-96751
ISBN 0-8034-9221-9

PRINTED IN THE UNITED STATES OF AMERICA
ON ACID-FREE PAPER
BY HADDON CRAFTSMEN, SCRANTON, PENNSYLVANIA

To Nancy Franklin, with many thanks
for your enthusiastic encouragement

Prologue

It was a dark, cloudy night, and the soft wind whipped Jan's wavy auburn hair around her face as she stood silently near the northeast corner of the house. She tilted her head to listen again for the sound that had caught her ears minutes before. The overgrown rhododendrons, tossing in the wind, produced a whispered chorus of their own, almost muffling other sounds. It seemed as though the hair on her neck stood up by itself, and she clutched her arms closely to her waist, gripping her elbows.

She turned her head from side to side, opening her brown eyes as widely as she could, trying to pick out any movement. The light of the moon and stars was almost nonexistent, hidden by the tumbling black clouds. There was the smell of rain, blowing in off the Pacific Ocean and across Puget Sound, seeking land it could soak, green growth to nourish.

The ten days she and the children had been living in this

1

old house, which was encompassed by overgrown rhodies and other shrubs and huge cedars and firs, and smaller alder, maple, and madrona trees, were too few to identify all sounds. The trees and shrubs gave the house beautiful, cool shade on a hot day, and a protecting arc for the cold wind, but tonight they made—and hid—unidentifiable noises, and provided hiding places for an unknown danger.

She backed up several steps, and as the clouds began delivering their promised rain, she felt movement behind her, entangling her, and she gave a choked scream.

Chapter One

When the opportunity had first come up three months earlier, in March, for Jan Gregg's sister, Char, to accompany her husband, Tom Trehearne, on his two-month assignment to New Zealand for a local software company, it had not looked possible. The ten-year-old twins could not go along. Normally Jan would have been pleased to offer to stay with the kids during the summer. As a schoolteacher, she and the children all had the summer off. However, she and Phyllis Bentsen, with whom she shared an apartment, vocation, shades of red hair, and long-term friendship, had planned a leisurely summer touring the British Isles.

To complicate the possibilities, Char and Tom had just signed closing papers on a ten-acre "farm" on Whidbey Island, complete with a seventy-year-old farmhouse, an unkempt old barn, chicken house, shed, well house, and a reasonable garage. Although Char and the kids were very excited about "the farm," Tom was less enthusiastic since it meant a longer commute for him, including a half-hour ferry ride morning and evening. But they had all agreed this was best for the family, and the move was set for mid-June, after school was out in Bellevue.

Char had told Jan about the farm with great enthusiasm. Her dark brown eyes, so like Jan's, had been bright with eagerness, because the five-bedroom, roomy old house, which admittedly needed considerable fixing up, would give her family room to spread out more. They were also anxious to get away from the city and its stressful aspects. Char had, however, spoken wistfully to Jan about going with Tom to New Zealand. Although they both loved the children dearly, this was a time in their marriage when they needed some time alone together.

As best-laid plans sometimes do, Jan's and Phyllis's ran into trouble when Phyllis slipped on the proverbial banana peel in the school cafeteria and broke her leg just four weeks before they were due to leave for England.

With Phyllis stuck in a cast and on crutches for at least eight to twelve weeks, they agreed sadly that it would be too difficult for Phyllis to do the British trip, which had included BritRailing, staying in bed-and-breakfast lodgings, and doing a great deal of walking as they toured, even some cross-country and coastal hiking. Although Phyllis encouraged Jan to go on her own, Jan flinched at the added cost and declared the trip would not be nearly as interesting and enjoyable alone. Fortunately they could cancel the airline tickets, and the travel insurance they had taken out covered their out-of-pocket expenses.

"Well, one good thing has come out of this," Jan teased Phyllis, who had just been helped up the stairs by their good-looking new neighbor, Roy Connors. "You finally got to meet the hunk!'' Phyllis had been trying to engineer a meeting with him since he'd moved in.

"Yes, I guess this was an ill wind that did blow *some* good. Although I would have met him sooner or later. Maybe,'' Phyllis said dreamily, "at the pool in my new swimsuit.'' Then she frowned. "Now I won't be able to wear it—or swim—all summer!'' she wailed.

Jan grinned, her brown eyes sparkling, "Sure you can *wear* it—you just won't be able to swim. But you can certainly do a good suntanning routine!''

The phone rang, and Jan crossed the living room to answer it. "Oh, hi, Char,'' she greeted her sister. "How are things?''

Char launched into a long-winded explanation of how, indeed, things were—practically a disaster waiting to happen, as they tried to get everything packed up to move. As Char talked, Jan got a thoughtful look on her face. Covering the phone's mouthpiece, she asked Phyllis, "Do you think you could manage here alone for a couple of months? Or, how would you like to spend some time on Whidbey Island?''

"Sure, I could manage fine.'' Phyll's eyes twinkled. "Especially now that I've met 'the hunk.' ''

"Char,'' Jan interrupted her sister, "Phyll's and my plans have changed. It looks like I'll be able to spend a couple of months with the twins on the island, and you can go to New Zealand with Tom.''

"What?'' her sister screeched, causing Jan to hold the phone a little distance from her ear. "What do you mean, I can go to New Zealand? What's happened? What do you mean?''

Launching into a humorous description of what had happened to Phyllis, Jan added, "But she got to meet the hunk at last! And he's not only good-looking, but he seems like a nice guy, too. Phyll is planning to cultivate his acquaintance this summer.'' She grinned at her roommate.

"Oh, Jan, I'm truly sorry about Phyll's accident and that you'll miss out on your trip to England. I know how much you were both looking forward to it. You've been planning it ever since you graduated from college three years ago!'' Then, rather reluctantly, Char added, "Are you sure you want to do this—stay with the kids for two whole months? There must be a lot of things you'd rather do.''

"No, I really want to do it, Char. You know the kids and I get along well, and you deserve a break from mothering—and some time just for you and Tom. Unless you think the kids will be unhappy with you gone?''

"They'll be thrilled and delighted to have you to themselves for a couple of months, Jan. You know you're their favorite aunt.''

"I'm their *only* aunt, at least locally,'' said Jan wryly, aware that the twins didn't know their Uncle Jim's wife, Renae, well at all since Jim and Renae lived in California. She ran her fingers through her tousled auburn curls as she listened to Char.

"Oh, Jan, I can't tell you how wonderful this is. How can I ever thank you? Tom will be so pleased!'' Char said excitedly.

"It's not too late for you to get your passport, is it?'' asked Jan. "I assume you want to fly over with Tom when he goes. When is that?''

"June fifteenth. School is out for the twins June tenth— when are you through?''

"Mine is over that day, too, although we teachers have to go in the next day to take care of some odds and ends.''

"The movers are coming early Saturday morning, the

twelfth, and since Tom's reservations are for the fifteenth, that's just a month from now. Wow!" Char exclaimed, "have I got a lot to do." She added hastily, "Are you *sure* you want to do this, Jan?"

Chuckling, Jan replied, "Yes, I'm sure I want to do this."

"Why don't you come over for dinner tonight and we can go over everything? Before you change your mind!" Char laughed. "Oh, no, wait—we have to sign the final papers for this house. How about tomorow night? Or won't that work?"

"No, I could probably do it tomorrow night—that would be the best night this week for me." Jan looked at Phyllis. "Will you be okay here alone tomorrow evening?"

Phyllis blushed. "Well, Roy said something about coming over . . ."

"Well, he *is* a fast worker!" Jan commented, then said to Char on the phone, "No problem. What time?"

After agreeing that six-thirty was agreeable, Jan hung up the phone. Phyllis looked at her curiously. "Are you sure you want to spend two entire months with two kids? Don't you get enough kids in the classroom?"

"Ah, but Trey and Tallie are different. They're my family, and they're ten years old—a wonderful age. Don't forget, for nine months a year I deal with teenagers, which is an entirely different kettle of fish!" Her expressive face, with its tip-tilted nose, reflected what kind of fish that kettle contained.

"Mmm, that's true. And the twins are nice kids."

"Anyway, I'm counting on frequent visits from you. Or," Jan said with a sly grin, "would you like to come spend the summer with us?"

"Uh-uh, you don't catch me that way. I want to see what

will happen with Roy, if anything. If he turns out to be only looks, then I may take you up on your offer." Phyllis was careful to hedge her bet. Jan noticed that Phyll was looking pale under her freckles. Her leg must be hurting.

"Well, you'll be welcome under any circumstances," Jan assured her. "Hey, I've got to run. I promised Diane I'd help with the senior tea tomorrow. That means she and I have a lot of work to do tonight getting ready. I'll see you later, Phyll. Is there anything I can do for you before I leave? Aspirin? Tea? Iced tea?"

Phyllis agreed that a glass of iced tea and some nibbles would be nice, and Jan got her comfortably ensconced on the couch with her leg propped up with plenty of pillows. She filled the ice pack and carefully placed it on Phyll's leg, and put the paper and some magazines within reach. She then went back to the school to help Diane, the home economics teacher, and assure her that everything would go well the next day. As it later turned out, the perpetual troublemaker of the senior class managed a first, no mean feat, and had spiked the punch when the chaperones weren't watching. Well, they couldn't exactly *prove* who had done it, but the consensus among the teachers was that it was Terri Fletcher. She had been clever enough, though, to not be caught, so she would graduate—with honors!— with her class.

Jan sat in the car for a few minutes after pulling into her sister's driveway. Char and Tom had bought this house in a nice Bellevue neighborhood when the kids were babies. The area had continued to build up rapidly since then and, indicative of the frenetic growth visible in most of the Puget Sound area, their street had become an unofficial thoroughfare for the new industrial park a mile away. Tom's commute across the lake to Seattle took twice as long (on a *good* day!) as it had nine years before. Although the commute from the farm would take a little longer, at least part of it would be a relaxed trip, with Tom sitting on the ferry. This would give him some time for his morning coffee and to read the paper—or do the extra work from the office he always seemed to have.

Tallie and Trey, ten-year-old blue-eyed, freckled blond dynamos, came racing around the side of the house, yelling to be heard over each other.

"AnJan! Hi—we're so glad you can make it for the summer!"

"Too bad you have to miss your trip to England, but we're sure glad you'll come to the farm with us!"

"Wait till you see it! It's really rad!"

"Come on in, we'll show you some pictures."

"AnJan, I helped Mom make the dessert—it's scrumptious!"

"Yuck! Don't you believe it! He can't cook!"

"Can too. I saw you trying to snitch some before dinner!"

"Starvation will make you eat anything!"

"Tallie, you take that back—or you can't have any dessert at all tonight, so there!"

Jan tried to restore order. "All right, kids, simmer down. Let's go in and see your creation, Trey. And Tallie, how about if you get those pictures out and show me your new house?" Jan stretched to her full five-feet-five after closing the car door. It had been a long day.

The kids had started calling her "AnJan" when they were small and it was difficult to add the extra syllables for "Aunt Janetta." Now, Trey asked, "AnJan, how's Phyll doing? Is she hurting much?"

"Not anymore. Her leg hurt quite a bit at first, and she still has to keep it propped up on a stool or pillow a lot and put an ice pack on it, but the way she gets around on her crutches now, you'd think she'd been born with them! But," Jan added hastily, in a warning tone lest the children think it sounded like fun, "she doesn't recommend getting around like that!"

As the three went through the side door, Char called out from the kitchen, "Hi, Jan. Tom's not home yet. Come have a cup of tea with me and let me pay homage to the person who has made possible my flight from pandemonium!" They hugged each other, and one could easily see the strong family resemblance, although Char's hair was more a reddish brown. "I can't begin to tell you how much Tom and I appreciate—"

"Hey, that's okay, Char. I understand; 'nuff said. Just mention me prominently in your will. I want the diamond earrings and the silver, please."

"Oh, no," said Tallie soberly, "Mom says I get the earrings, and Trey and I share the silver!"

"I know, honey," said Jan, "I was only teasing." She laughed, her dimples showing.

Tallie followed them into the kitchen. "Here are the pictures, AnJan." She eagerly laid them on the kitchen table under the skylight. Quickly opening the photograph envelope, she started spreading out the pictures. "Look, here's the house from the front. See this window upstairs? That's Mom and Dad's room. Trey and I have rooms looking out the back, toward the barn and pasture. Isn't that fab?" Jan nodded, oohing and ahhing appropriately.

Trey broke in, "See, here's the old barn. Dad says we'll probably have to pull it down, but Tallie and I don't want him to. It would be a great place to play, and we want to have horses, and a cow, and chickens and ducks. Look— there's a pond in back! Don't you think that would be a great place for ducks and geese? And a dog and cat—those come first!"

Jan looked at Char mischievously. "It appears this is going to be a *working* farm, doesn't it? Got your gum boots yet, Char?"

Char rolled her hazel eyes. "They have big ideas, but they have no idea how much work all those animals would be. I do agree about the dog though, especially out in the country that way. Besides, with ten acres, we shouldn't have to keep him penned up."

Trey broke in, "Me and Tallie could take care of the animals. We'd get up early before school and feed and water everything."

"Yeah," Tallie concurred, "that would be really neat! I want a palomino horse, all gold and silver. And a fancy saddle with lots of silver trim . . ."

"Whoa, there, kids! These are things we have yet to talk about, and we'd need a lot more information before adding an entire menagerie," Char interrupted. "Please don't expect too much. All your father and I are agreeing to at this point is a dog."

"It all sounds good to me," Jan said, tongue in cheek.

"Don't encourage them, Jan, please!" Char admonished. "And," she added sternly, "I don't want to come back from New Zealand and find the farm full of livestock!"

"Not likely," retorted Jan. "I don't know much about anything but dogs and cats, so I'm not about to populate your property while you're gone. It would be nice, though," she said wistfully, "to come visit later on and enjoy all those animals."

"Bite your tongue!" said Char, while Trey and Tallie

cheered her on. "Not that *you* won't be welcome, but you may just have to settle for humans!"

Tom arrived home just then, and following the hug and kiss for Char and the hair-tousling and hugs for the twins, Tom gave Jan a big hug, expressing his gratitude with a "Thanks, kid! You're all right!"

Dinner was lively, with the pictures being passed around and an ongoing discussion of how the house would be updated. Some rooms were to be combined, and the kitchen and bathroom modernized with installation of a second bathroom high on the priority list. They agreed the old orchard had great possibilities, and Char described how the huge old lilac trees had been in bloom when they first looked at the property, obviously a selling point for her. The twins continued to push for a full range of animals.

Before Jan left, it was agreed that she would make the trip to Whidbey Island with her sister's family that coming Sunday so she could see her summer home and, also important, learn "how to get there from here." Char and Tom were insistent that they pay her at least a little something for her time and efforts, as well, of course, as paying all the expenses while they were gone. "This way I won't feel so guilty asking you to do some unpacking and stuff," Char said with a cheeky grin. "Besides, you deserve far more just for staying with the kids! They can be rather wearing on a full-time basis."

"They'll behave themselves or I'll beat them with the big stick I use on the kids in class," Jan warned, scowling ferociously at the twins.

"Aw, AnJan," Trey interjected, "we know you wouldn't do that!"

"Yeah," Tallie added knowingly, "you've stayed with us lots of times, and you're always nice."

"More like a pushover," said Tom in an aside.

"But you've only been with me for a few hours, or maybe a day or two at a time," Jan responded. "My students could tell you that on a daily basis, I can be really tough!"

"Somehow I think this will be a learning experience for all of you," Tom commented. "I just hope it doesn't turn you off marriage and a family permanently, Jan!"

"Dad, couldn't we at least get some chickens or ducks or somethin' while you're gone? They wouldn't be much work, would they? Or how about some goats? They eat *anything!*" Trey begged eagerly. "They'd be lots of help cleaning up all those blackberry vines and stuff. We could have a lot of the yard and field cleaned up by the time you get back."

Tallie added her two cents' worth. "And a horse! Horses eat a lot of grass and stuff—he'd hardly cost anything!"

Tom looked at Char. "What have we wrought here?" he asked solemnly. "I think we may have unleashed a monster—or monsters. I thought all we wanted was some fresh air and a little elbow room!"

"Honey, you know all little girls want a horse." She smiled at Tallie but admonished both children, "You'll just have to wait for any of that until we get back. It's not fair to ask AnJan to cope with anything like that."

Jan heaved an exaggerated sigh of relief. "Saved by the bell! Kids, I wouldn't have any idea how to take care of a horse. Why don't we try for a garden instead?" They dubiously agreed to consider a garden, but only peas, potatoes, and onions—and perhaps tomatoes.

That night, while they slept, several events were taking place that would have an effect on their lives. In a downtown Seattle office building, a group of agents representing two countries, two states, several counties, and a number of agencies from them, met again with grim faces to discuss ways and means of stopping the increased drug trafficking, especially of the dangerous new ''China white'' heroin, in the northwestern United States and southwestern Canada. Although some drugs came across the land border between the two countries, most came in by boat—freighters, pleasure boats, luxury liners—on almost anything that can float.

They were discussing a strong tip that had been received earlier that day concerning drugs coming ashore on Whidbey Island, apparently somewhere between Coupeville and Oak Harbor. The map on the wall was dotted with a number of colored pins, and the discussion went far into the night. Finally a plan was drawn up. Among other things, agents would be based in various locations, with believable cover stories, to keep watch on activities in their area. It would be impossible to be everywhere, so they chose what they thought the most likely sites. The line would be spread thin, but they felt it was the best they could do with available resources.

During the next few days, agents were chosen, briefed, and put in place. The watching began.

And on the other side of the Pacific, plans for increased shipments were going forward to breach those defenses.

Jan and Char had grown up just north of Seattle, in Lynnwood, and had gone to school there. Char married two years into her college career, when Tom graduated from the University of Washington. Jan, however, was determined to finish college, become a teacher, and do some traveling before she looked around for a mate. Although she knew deep in her heart that if ''the right man'' came along she would probably change her mind, she was still heart-whole and fancy free at twenty-five.

Over the years, she'd had a number of boyfriends, many of whom she still considered friends. The previous winter she'd dated Bob Bradley, a fellow teacher, quite a bit; but a new blond substitute teacher had caught his eye. Although Jan was a little miffed about it—who doesn't want to be the one to break it off?—she was not really unhappy, knowing nothing serious would have come of the relationship. Bob was fun, good-looking, and would make someone a great husband—but not Jan!

Slim and moderately athletic, Jan enjoyed her work with the teenagers in her high school classes. Her specialty was history, with a minor in American literature. A fairly good swimmer, golfer, and skier, Jan felt she lived in the most beautiful part of the world.

After Bob had defected to the cute blond, Jan determined to make some changes in her life, one of which was having her long auburn hair cut shorter to emphasize her thick-lashed brown eyes. Another change was to have been the trip to England with Phyllis. When that fell through, it seemed better to spend the time with the twins so Char could have a special summer. Hanging around the city did not appeal to her, even though there were many things to do, alone and with friends. She and Phyll had agreed to continue saving their money and try for England the following summer. A summer on Whidbey Island with the twins would be a change for Jan, she thought. *And at least I can enjoy some fresh country air. . . .*

Chapter Two

A month later, Jan and the twins were settled in the old farmhouse and were busy cleaning the kitchen cabinets so they could reline the shelves and unpack and put away the dishes and glassware. Outside, the western Washington weather was doing what it did best and frequently—drizzling. It seldom really rained in western Washington, but it was very good at misting, drizzling, and very gently depositing light drops of rain on everything. Not often was there a thunderstorm. Frequently, there was just one large gray cloud from horizon to horizon, raining softly, intermittently.

The twins had been very disappointed to awaken to a wet morning, but Jan chivied them along to breakfast and the current project of unwrapping dishes, washing and lining the cupboard shelves, and filling them. "Just think how pleased your mother will be not to have to do this when she gets back. Besides, we do need dishes for eating!"

"We could use paper plates and plastic glasses, forks, and spoons," Tallie suggested. "Then we wouldn't have so many dishes to wash! We could just throw them away," she continued eagerly.

"Yeah," added Trey. "It would be like camping. It sure *seems* like a camp in the woods with all the trees and bushes around the house."

"We'll find something fun to do this afternoon," Jan said. "We could walk down to the beach—that's not far. Perhaps the rain will even stop after lunch. Or," she said enthusiastically, "if we get the rest of these boxes unpacked and the rain stops before lunch, we can take some sandwiches with us and eat by the water!"

The twins both liked that idea and turned to the unpacking with more zeal than previously, although eyeing the sky dubiously. Knowing children so well, Jan gave them a break mid-morning, along with some cocoa, apples, crackers, and cheese. The twins pulled every knock-knock joke they could recall on Jan, who went along with them as though she'd never heard the jokes before. Then back to work for a couple of more hours, when Jan finally called a halt after much begging from the kids.

"Okay, let's pack a lunch—I can see you're both hot to trot! What shall we take for lunch?"

"Bologna sandwiches!" "Peanut butter and jelly sandwiches!" they chimed in unison.

"Okay, you each fix the sandwich you want, plus an extra half sandwich for me. Add some fruit and a bag of chips, too, and pack them up in those little plastic bags, please," Jan instructed. "I'll run up to my room to find my knapsack and see if I can find my canteen, too, and we'll take something to drink in that, okay?"

"Coke!" "Pepsi!" Each indicated his and her choice.

"How about milk?" Groans from the twins. "Okay, we can always settle for water—that's usually what a canteen contains anyway." The twins just stared at her, and they finally all agreed on lemonade.

By the time they were ready to leave, the sky was showing scattered patches of blue. Jan smiled, her eyes twinkling. "My grandma—your great-grandma—used to say that if there was a patch of blue sky big enough to make a pair of Dutchman's britches, it was going to clear up."

"Yeah?" Tallie giggled. "He must be a pretty big man!"

"Did it hafta be one big patch of blue? Or could you take a lot of blue *patches* and sew them together for his pants?" Trey asked, emphasizing the words to show he was making a joke, at which his aunt and sister both groaned. Jan sketched a "one" in the air to show he'd scored a point.

Jan tucked the back door key in her jeans pocket, with the forest-green knapsack containing their lunch on her back, as they left and started around the side of the old house. "I'll bet this is pretty in the springtime when all the rhodies are in bloom," she exclaimed. "And you can see there have been lots of daffodils. You know," she added, "we really need to do something about cutting down some of this grass and weeds. I wonder if there's anyone in the neighborhood who could come mow it down for us."

Trey puffed out his chest. "I can do it," he boasted. "When the grass dries out some, I'll get the mower out of the shed and start on it."

"I don't know, Trey," demurred Jan. "It's terribly tall and thick. I think we should have someone in with a really big mower the first time, and then you—and Tallie—can keep it down after that." She added quickly, at the frown on his face as he started to object that he was big and strong enough to do it, "Frankly, I don't think our mower would manage it, and it would be a shame to break the machine. Just think," she said, tongue in cheek, "then we wouldn't be able to mow the rest of the summer!"

Trey laughed at her. "Tough, huh?"

They crossed the road that looped back to join the main road a mile north of them. There was a strong family resemblance among them, even though the twins were blue-eyed blonds and Jan a brown-eyed redhead, with all of them in blue jeans and sweatshirts. Jan's beige sweatshirt read, *Life's too short not to eat popcorn,* and had a sketch of a big bowl of buttered popcorn on it. They walked about two hundred feet along the road, then started down a gravel road that led to the beach. It was a gradual slope with a slight curve, and soon they were looking out over the Strait of Juan de Fuca. Off to their right, forming the northern boundary of the Strait, was Vancouver Island, Canada. There were several freighters and a big tanker within view, as well as a Navy frigate steaming into Admiralty Inlet, thence to the new Navy base on Elliott Bay in Everett. A small boat ramp was off to their left, with a couple of cars parked nearby. There were houses to the right and left, but some distance away from the boat ramp, which was on a small slice of public land. There was a decrepit old picnic table there and an overflowing trash receptacle.

"Wow!" breathed Tallie. "Look at all that water—and those boats and stuff . . . Look! There's some guys fishin' over there—and one of them's caught something!"

"Can we go fishin', AnJan?" Trey piped up. "That looks cool! Then we could have fish for dinner!"

"And you're such wonderful little fish eaters," Jan commented dryly. "I think it would be easier to buy some at the store."

"Aw, AnJan, that's no fun! We could probably rent a boat," enthused Trey, "and go out there on the Sound. Hey, maybe we could catch enough to sell some. Maybe enough to buy our *own* boat! I think I want to be a fisherman when I get big," he said, embroidering on the theme.

"Me, too," said Tallie, then added dubiously, "I think."

They left the road and clambered across and around the logs that had been cast onto the pebbly beach by the tide over the years. Although the environmentalists had succeeded in sharply eliminating much of the logging that had been one of the backbone industries for Washington State in past decades, most Puget Sound beaches were still lined with logs that had escaped the log booms that for many years traversed the area's rivers and the Sound. Some logs were so far from normal high tide that only extreme, storm-driven waves would be able to drag them back to the cold, celadon-green water. Others were damp and sandy, indicating that the tide regularly shifted their bulk.

The twins went straight down to the water, and Jan automatically warned, "Be careful, don't get your shoes wet!"

Trey exclaimed, "Look, there's crabs here," and bent down to turn over a rock. "Look out, there he goes!"

Tallie screeched, "Keep him away from me!" And then, as Trey picked up the small crab and chased after her, she ran toward Jan. "Don't let him get near me with that, AnJan! Eek!" she squealed as the cold water on Trey's hand and the crab splattered on her.

"Now stop that, Trey! Don't try to scare your sister!"

"I'm not scared," Tallie quavered. "I just don't want to be pinched!"

But it wasn't long before both children were chasing crabs and oohing and ahhing over some starfish in a small tidal pool and gathering shells and colorful pebbles from the beach. Jan strolled with them, enjoying the fresh salt air and the beautiful view. The sun peeked out from time to time, highlighting both red and gold lights in her wind-tousled hair. *What a wonderful place to live,* she thought to herself. *Lucky Char! I wonder if I could find a place near here? On the other hand, it would be a long commute when school's in session. Hmm—I wonder if I could get a job in one of the school districts on the island? There's a thought! But that would leave Phyllis stuck with the apartment on her own.*

Later they hungrily consumed their lunch at the picnic table near the boat ramp. "Hey, AnJan," Trey piped up. "We forgot to bring some dessert!"

"I thought perhaps we'd make some chocolate chip cookies when we go back to the house. How does that sound?" The twins were delighted with that plan, but weren't ready yet to return to the house. They gathered up their trash and put it in one of the plastic bags, then into the knapsack, so they could dispose of it when they returned to the house. The trash bin was too full to add to.

As they walked northward along the beach, they came to some scattered homes. Some were small beach cottages, but further on were several large homes, each with the side facing the westward view lined with large, shiny glass windows. Each house had its own character, enhanced by the variety of windows, decks, and colors, with a minimum of landscaping showing on the sea side.

"This is probably private beachfront," Jan remarked, "so we'd better turn back."

"Aw, we're not hurtin' anything," Trey grumbled.

"No, but if you lived in one of these houses, you wouldn't want everyone and his spotted pup coming along just any old time, would you?"

"Well, no, I guess not, AnJan. Can we walk back down the beach the other way?"

"Sure, for a short distance. Look—there's a fisherman coming back in. Do you suppose he's caught something for his dinner?" They headed south along the beach.

When they got closer, they could see a tall, husky man going through the process of tying everything down on the boat before towing it out of the water. He wore a blue plaid shirt and loden down vest, and his dark brown hair was rumpled from the wind, his tanned face indicating a lot of time spent outdoors.

Jan blinked her heavily fringed brown eyes and thought to herself, *Hey, not bad! Is this where all the good-looking guys live? Maybe I should move to the island!*

"Hey, mister, can I see your fish?" Trey dashed forward. "We saw you out there on the boat! How many did you catch? What kind are they?" He eyed the two salmon the man had on a stringer line.

"Hey, whoa there," Jan said. "That's not being very polite, Trey. Perhaps this gentleman would rather not be bothered."

The man smiled slightly, his dark blue eyes . . . wary? "No problem, ma'am. You know how fishermen are—always ready to brag about their catch!"

"I thought that was usually about those that got away." Jan smiled, her dimples flashing. He wasn't exactly handsome but had the rugged, craggy looks that often were far more attractive. Probably thirty or so, and no ring visible on his left hand. She sighed at the reflex check a single woman learns early on.

The children crowded closer, with Jan standing back a bit. "Ooh, look, AnJan," Tallie squeaked. "How big they are!" She drew back when the man held the fish closer so she could touch it, which she did, but very gingerly. "Ooh, ick! It's all slimy and yucky!"

"No, it's not!" exclaimed Trey, also touching it. "It's just slippery—really smooth! Come on and touch it, AnJan!"

"Uh, I think I'll take a rain check," replied Jan, wrinkling up her nose.

"Aw, AnJan, don't be a sissy!"

Jan raised her eyebrows and threw up her hands with a "what can I do" look at the man. He held the fish closer, his eyes twinkling. "They really don't bite, ma'am—at least not after they're out of the water," he assured her in his deep voice.

Ma'am? thought Jan. *I'm not old enough to be a ma'am!*

Tallie spoke up. "We just moved in up the hill—into the old Peterson place. I'm Tallie Trehearne, and this is my brother, Trey; actually, Thomas the third, but we call him Trey. We're twins, you know! We've been unpacking dishes and stuff all morning, and then we came down and had a picnic. Trey caught a crab and chased me with it," she said complainingly. "And we saw some starfish, and took a walk up the beach. . . . What's your name, mister? Do you live around here? Do you have any kids?" She paused to take a breath.

He hesitated, nonplussed, and looked at Jan, who grinned at his discomfiture. "Cade—uh, Colby. Up the beach a ways," he said, waving vaguely to the south. "Does she do that all the time?" he asked Jan. "Talk without breathing?"

She responded, "Frequently. Both of them, as a matter

of fact.'' She smiled up at him, ''I'm Jan Gregg, aunt to these two.'' She wasn't sure if he was being friendly or merely polite, but she held out her hand to shake his.

He held her hand for a long moment, his dark blue eyes looking deeply into hers. Her hand felt very small and soft in his large, rough one. His touch sent a surprising tingle through her before she pulled her hand out of his grip and looked away, at the children.

He grinned, then looked at the twins and said, ''I'll tell you what, kids. If you think you'd like some salmon for dinner, I'll give you one of these fish.''

''Oh, no,'' Jan said, ''I'm sure your family is looking forward to fresh fish for dinner and freezing the rest for the winter.'' *Maybe no ring, but let's double-check,* she thought.

The creases beside his mouth indented slightly, showing a flash of white in the tanned face. ''No family, just me, and one fish will be plenty for me, I assure you.''

''Oh, please, AnJan, just think how good it will be! You can fix it with that stuff Mom uses that's so good,'' urged Tallie.

The man's eyes gleamed at this reminder that Jan was indeed not mother to the twins. *Ah,* he thought, *and no ring on her finger. Very nice!* Then he caught himself up. *Don't even* think *of her that way—you've got a job to do here!*

''You mean with dill? Hmm, that would taste good,'' replied Jan. ''Are you sure you don't mind parting with one of the fish, sir? Perhaps I could pay you for it.''

His voice turned a little brusque. ''No, you can't pay me for it.'' He shrugged. ''If you don't want it . . .''

Jan blushed a little. ''I'm sorry, I didn't mean to offend you. And yes, we'd be delighted to have salmon for dinner. Thank you.''

Trey piped up, "Hey, AnJan, why don't we invite Cade to dinner? You said we'd make chocolate chip cookies when we get home, and I'll bet he likes 'em too!"

Before Jan could comment one way or the other, Cade excused himself. "Thanks for the thought, Trey, but I have some work to do. Here," he said as he detached the smaller fish from the stringer and held it out to Jan.

"Uh . . ." Jan clearly didn't want to take the slippery fish in her hands. "Wait." She pulled the knapsack off her back. "There's a plastic bag in here that we could put it in. . . ." She emptied the lunch debris into the knapsack in order to use the largest plastic bag in there. She held it open as Cade slipped the salmon into it. "Thanks so much." She smiled. "We'll really enjoy this. And then," she said, grinning at Trey, "we'll have a better idea if you really *do* want to become a fisherman!"

When she looked up, Cade was already turning away. He flashed them a smile and waved at them. "See you . . ." he said casually as he got into his car to tow the boat out of the water.

" 'Bye," Trey and Tallie chorused. "We'll see you soon!"

Jan looked after him with puzzlement in her eyes, wondering why he'd left so abruptly. Well, maybe he didn't like kids—or strangers. . . . Or maybe he didn't like red hair? But her hand still tingled, and when she looked back a few minutes later, as they climbed the hill, she noticed him look up from fastening the boat trailer to the hitch on the car and look after them. She smiled faintly to herself, slightly comforted by that look.

The twins chattered all the way back up the hill about Cade and the fish. *It certainly doesn't take much to impress a couple of kids.* Jan thought, admitting ironically, *or me!*

As the children wondered aloud about how long Cade had lived on the island and how often he went fishing, Jan, too, silently wondered.

"Do you suppose he'd take me fishing sometime?" Trey asked Jan.

"Whoa there, Trey, we just met the man for a few minutes. Just because he gave us a fish doesn't mean he wants to get acquainted with us."

"I don't know, AnJan," commented Tallie. "But he was sure looking at you!"

"Honey, he looked at all three of us," Jan responded in exasperation.

"Not like he looked at you!" Tallie retorted.

"Your imagination is working overtime," Jan commented. "Hey, does anyone know how to clean salmon?"

None of them did. Jan had a vague idea of the process but wasn't sure. Stumped for a while, she finally called the meat and fish department at the local supermarket and asked. The department manager laughed but kindly explained the process. It wasn't a pretty sight, but with a sharp knife in her hand and a look of distaste on her face, Jan did what was necessary. Cade or any other fisherman would probably have shuddered at the process and the looks of the finished product, but Jan figured it couldn't have tasted any better if it had been cleaned by a professional.

That day set something of a routine for the following days. They spent some time in the mornings unpacking various things, and Jan helped each of the children get their rooms in some order. This made them feel more at home. They frequently all walked down to the water together, as Jan did not feel comfortable having them go there on their own. This caused some disagreement from the twins, who felt they were old enough to go on their own. Jan contended that since she was responsible for them, they would do it her way. When their parents returned, she told them, the twins could take it up with Char and Tom. "Don't forget, we still don't know many people around here, and you don't know who might be on the beach when you're there, especially with the boat ramp there. That's it—no more discussion!"

They saw Cade Colby several times, but he was usually out on his boat although one time he was going into the fifth cottage along, a gray one with white shutters. He waved back at them, and Jan could see the flash of white as he smiled, and wished he was on the beach sometimes when they came down. Early one evening they saw him turn out of the gravel road in his black, four-door vehicle that Trey identified as a Ford Bronco. He waved but did not stop.

Unless it rained, Jan and the twins spent a lot of time in the yard and pasture, with the children reluctantly agreeing that until new fencing could be installed, there was no way to keep larger animals in. The old chicken coop was dirty and dusty and would also need much done to it before new lodgers could live there, and when Tallie and Jan saw the mouse and rat droppings, they got out quickly, agreeing that chickens could wait. Jan enjoyed identifying some of the shrubs and flowers that were blooming, had already bloomed, or would do so later in the summer.

There was an old, long-established bed of iris that badly needed thinning. Several old-fashioned rosebushes were blooming with colorful abandon in pink, white, and dark red, and a yellow climbing rosebush almost covered the roof of the well house. Yellow and tangerine daylilies lined the edge of the front yard along the ditch, and a pink and yellow honeysuckle sprawled along the pasture fence, sending sweet fragrance abroad at twilight.

When their parents called Saturday evening, the children bubbled over, taking turns to inform them of all they had been doing. Jan spoke to them briefly, conscious of the expense of the already lengthy conversation. She assured her sister and brother-in-law that they were managing very well, pointing out that she'd found someone to come in with a big riding mower to cut the grass down to where their mower could take over. She was pleased to hear that not only was the business end of the trip going well, but that Char and Tom were enjoying the time together in beautiful New Zealand.

The children were a little quiet after their parents had hung up, so Jan suggested popping some corn and watching an often-watched but much-loved Disney movie. By the time the drowsy children were popped into bed, Jan was ready for some time alone. She went along to heat some water for a cup of tea and raided the cookie jar to see if the twins had overlooked any, then settled down for an hour's quiet reading of a new historical novel she'd brought with her.

Sunday, as the three were out exploring, they had an opportunity to meet the neighbors to the south of them. Although they knew from the mailbox that the family name was Norris and that two horses lived in that pasture, they had not seen anyone around during the day, although at night there was usually a light or two in the house. Today, however, they met Cheryl Norris and her two children, Robby, age eleven, and Emily, age nine. They had just returned from a two-week visit to Cheryl's mother in Oregon. The children hit it off at once, and Emily and Robby excitedly invited the twins to meet the horses, Slap and Happy.

Jan explained why she was staying two months with the twins and assured Cheryl she'd like Char and Tom. She and Cheryl had a nice visit, with Cheryl offering help and/ or information whenever Jan needed it. "When you live out in the country like this, neighbors are important," she added.

She spent the next hour filling Jan in on some of the other neighbors, the local school, and life in general on Whidbey Island, until Jan apologized, saying, "I didn't mean to take up so much of your time. I'm sure you have things to do after being gone so long."

"Oh, no problem—it'll keep!" Cheryl's merry dark eyes and small, pointed chin gave her a gamine look. She was obviously a happy woman who enjoyed life.

Tallie and Trey were reluctant to be parted so soon from their new friends. Cheryl invited them to stay on for a couple more hours. Jan was pleased at how well the children hit it off and that their ages were close together. Hopefully they would become good friends over time.

That afternoon Jan was doing more unpacking for her sister. The kids were outside wandering around, but about mid-afternoon they suddenly ran in the back way, slamming the door.

With one look at them, Jan asked, "What's wrong?"

"Nothing . . ." Trey began.

"It's that man . . ." said Tallie.

"What man? Where? Did he hurt you?"

"He yelled at us!" Tallie said indignantly. "Said to get off his land!"

Trey pointed to the north, where the next house was the equivalent of three or four blocks away, with most of the

Trehearne pasture, then some woods and another clear patch before the neighboring house, a small, shabby brown cedar-shingled cottage. "The fence is down, y'know?" Jan nodded as she put an arm around Tallie, who was still shaking. "Well," Trey added reluctantly, "we decided to look in the woods—sorta playing cowboys and Indians, y'know?" He stopped and swallowed.

"Yes?" Jan encouraged as she reached out a hand to stroke back Trey's rumpled blond curls.

"Well, all of a sudden, there's this old geezer, with a big stick in his hand, yelling at us to get off his land, that he don't allow no trespassin', and didn't we see the sign?"

Tallie spoke up, "He sure was ugly and mean-lookin', Jan! Boy, did we get out of there quick! We ran all the way home!"

"Well, of course you shouldn't have been trespassing, but there was no need for him to be so nasty. Maybe I should go talk to him. . . ."

"I don't think so, AnJan—he sure didn't look like he'd listen to *anyone!* And he must be at least a hundred years old!" Trey interrupted.

"Hmm . . . You know, I think I'll call Cheryl Norris and ask her about him. I remember she mentioned that an old man lived there, but if he's dangerous, we should know. On the other hand, perhaps he's just a cranky old man who doesn't like children."

She called Cheryl and told her what had happened. Cheryl laughed wryly. "Oh, that's Old Henry Horne, Jan. Don't worry, his bark is worse than his bite. He never has a nice word to say to anyone, and I've never seen him smile. If you leave him alone, he'll leave you alone." Then she continued, a smile in her voice, "When we first moved here, I thought I'd be a good neighbor and take him a pie—

just to get acquainted. He slammed the door in my face.'' She laughed, then asked, ''Are the kids okay? I hope they weren't too frightened. I've never heard of him hurting any-one—he's just grumpy.''

Jan felt better and thanked Cheryl. ''I wasn't sure if I should go down there and confront him or what. He certainly made an impression on the twins!''

''I imagine so. We don't see him out and about very often. He's not exactly a hermit, but he *is* a loner. I think he's been there almost as long as Mrs. Peterson lived in your house. They were both old-timers around here. I suppose with just Mrs. Peterson in your place for so many years, he's used to not having anyone come on his property from your direction. Some of the neighborhood kids used to give him a bad time at Halloween. Three years ago, he threatened them with a shotgun! One of the deputy sheriffs went by and warned him about that, but he also put the word out to the kids in the area to leave Old Henry alone. It's possible some of them have been harassing him, though, and he took it out on your kids.''

''You can be sure they'll stay away from there from now on! They were really scared when they came running in the house,'' said Jan, ''which of course scared me. Thanks so much for filling me in,'' she added. ''If Char and her family had been living here for a while, she would have warned me. Are there any other neighborhood characters I should know about?''

''Not that I know of, but of course people come and go along the beach. Except for the boat ramp, most of it is private, but that doesn't stop people from wandering around. We really haven't had many problems, however.''

Jan thanked her again, hung up, and repeated most of the conversation to the children. ''I guess I don't have to warn you to stay on our property, do I?'' she asked, and was eagerly assured they would never go into Mr. Horne's woods again.

That evening, about an hour after the children had gone to bed, Jan was feeling restless. She put down the book she had been reading. It was a warm evening, and she could smell the fragrance of the honeysuckle floating on the still air. Off in the distance came a rumble of thunder. The clouds had been thickening late in the afternoon, promising rain to come. On impulse she stepped out through the back screen door, smiling with pleasure at the intensified scent of honeysuckle. From the west came a lightning flash, followed several seconds later by a rumble of thunder.

Perhaps we're going to get a thunderstorm here tonight, she thought. Very little light shone through the back door, as she hadn't bothered turning on a light in the kitchen. She wandered toward the honeysuckle-draped fence, glad that the grass had been mowed. From the direction of the pond came the garrumping and ribbiting of frogs, and the wind rustled through the trees, quickening as the storm neared. From the corner of her eye, Jan thought she saw a gleam of light near the barn, but just then lightning flashed across the sky, and she wasn't sure if she had indeed seen anything.

A little tense, she turned back toward the house, suddenly aware of their isolation, with herself out in the middle of the yard. As the thunder's rumble faded away, Jan heard a sound near the barn, a sharp thump, as of wood against wood. She stopped and stood still as a statue, straining her ears for another sound, but heard only the sound of the rhododendrons and trees tossing in the freshening wind. She tilted her head and opened her eyes as widely as she could, staring in the barn's direction. Because of the clouds, there was no light from the moon and stars, and the faint light from the back door was quickly swallowed by the darkness.

As she backed toward the house, lightning flashed overhead, followed closely by a clap of thunder, and the clouds began to deliver the threatened rain. A few more steps . . . Jan gave a muffled yelp as she felt movement behind her, entangling her, until she realized it was the rhododendrons, buffeted by the rising wind. She whirled and ran to the back door, dashing in and slamming shut the door and locking it. Her heart was beating rapidly. She quickly closed the door into the dining room, shutting out the light, and returned to look out the back door's window to see if she saw any light, debating whether or not to call the sheriff's office. She stood there for a long time without seeing any sign of a light, finally deciding she must have imagined it and that the sound she had heard had been a wild animal of some sort, or perhaps the wind had blown something over. She knew there were deer, coyotes, rabbits, and racoons, as well as bats and owls, at night.

"Tomorrow we're getting a dog!" she declared forcefully, carefully locking doors and windows before going to bed.

Her suggestion the next morning to the children about getting a dog was met with delighted enthusiasm. "We'll get the local paper and see if anyone is trying to find a good home for a dog," she suggested. "Or"—inspiration struck—"perhaps the local vet will know about a dog needing a home. I remember my friend Lacey getting her dog that way."

Jan checked the phone book for the nearest veterinarian

and discovered they needed to pass her clinic on their way to town to get a paper, so they decided to make that their first stop. They hurried through breakfast, discussing what kind of dog they'd get and what they'd name him. "Or her," added Tallie.

When they went into the veterinary clinic's office, Jan explained their mission. The receptionist gestured to the bulletin board on a side wall, covered with various notices. Some were for pedigreed dogs and cats for sale, and some were for animals looking for homes. One really stood out: WANTED: *Good home for four-year-old brindle Great Dane. Reasonably good guard dog but wonderful with children. Free to good home. Has been through obedience training.* It gave the phone number to call.

"Hey, AnJan, a Great Dane! Wouldn't that be great?" Trey said excitedly.

"I don't know; they're awfully big; he might be rough— and he must eat a lot!"

"But it says 'wonderful with children,' " Tallie entreated.

"Yeah, and he'd already know to ask to go out to do his duty," added Trey. "And Tallie and I will take care of him—feed him, and brush him, and bathe him."

Jan's mind boggled at the idea of bathing a Great Dane. On the other hand, a Great Dane would certainly have a loud bark and would scare away intruders—if there indeed ever were any—and it did say he was a good guard dog. "Well, I guess we could call about him." She turned to the receptionist and asked, "Are you at all familiar with this Great Dane who needs a home?"

"Oh, yes, he comes in for his shots and things. A very easygoing, affectionate animal. His owners, Dick and Audrey Sawley, are in the Navy and being transferred to Kodiak, Alaska, and are afraid that would be too difficult for the dog." She added, "If you like, I'll call the Sawleys to see if they still have him."

The twins turned pleading eyes to Jan. "Well, I guess that wouldn't hurt."

Almost before she knew it, they were on their way to Oak Harbor to see the animal. When she saw him, she blanched. "This isn't a dog, it's a pony! What will your parents say if they come home to find him there?" But he obviously was good with children. Mrs. Sawley was regretful at having to part with their pet, but not only would they be living in an apartment when they got to Kodiak, but they were also expecting their first baby. "He's sort of been our 'baby' up to now," she said, "but it wouldn't be fair to him to take him up there. He's been used to having a yard to run in, and up there, he wouldn't have that freedom—only an apartment."

So by lunchtime, they were all home again with the new addition to the family. "If I had known his name was Tiger," Jan muttered, "I might never have gone there in the first place. That's a very dangerous-sounding name." The children were thrilled, however, and wanted to take him outside to play right away. "You'd better keep him on the leash for a few days," Jan warned, "until he's familiar with the area."

Mrs. Sawley had sent along all his dishes, toys, his cedar-filled bed, a box of large dog bones, and an enormous bag of dog food. Jan had to admit that the brown-and-black brindling did lend itself to the name Tiger—and that he was a very affectionate animal. "I just hope he's a good watchdog," she mused as she put things away and prepared lunch.

* * *

That afternoon they decided to take Tiger for a walk down to the beach, with the twins hoping he'd chase sticks for them. He seemed quite well mannered, so Trey decided to take the leash off. This worked fine for a while, and they discovered Tiger liked to chase seagulls along the beach and into the shallow water. They saw Cade out on his boat. *Does that man never work? He's always out fishing! Hmm . . . Perhaps he works nights, or is on vacation,* Jan mused.

When Cade brought his boat in, Tiger spotted him and galloped off to meet him. "Tiger, come back," they all called in varying tones of voice and command, but he obviously intended to satisfy his curiosity about this other human.

When Tiger came woofing nearer, Cade turned quickly, his eyes widening at the size of the dog. He saw who was chasing after the dog and assumed the dog to be friendly, but cautiously held out his hand, palm down, for the dog to sniff. Tiger's tail was wagging furiously, a doggy grin on his face. "Okay," said Cade, "so you're a friendly so-and-so, are you?"

Looking up at Jan and the twins, he commented, "Looks like you've been adopted by a horse!"

The twins chattered away about the dog and how wonderful he was. "And he's good with children, too," Tallie pointed out. "Mrs. Sawley says so."

Cade looked at Jan over their heads and grinned. "Yeah, he's so friendly he'll probably knock someone down with his tail if you're not careful!"

"One look and they were goners," Jan replied. "I really hadn't intended to get such a large animal, but he does have a good-sized voice on him. Old buildings have so many noises . . ."

His gaze sharpened. "Why, have you been hearing strange noises?"

She glanced at the children, but they were fully involved with Tiger, looking for another stick to toss for him. "Well . . . I don't know. You know that storm last night?" He nodded. "Well, before it came in, I went out in the backyard. The kids were asleep, and I was getting ready to lock up for the night. But the honeysuckle and roses smelled so lovely, and it was quite warm, so I just sort of stepped out the door and then down the steps. Things were quiet, except for occasional thunder." She paused.

"Go on," he said, his voice gruff, his eyes ranging over her expressive face.

"Well, I don't know that I *did* see or hear anything—it was probably just the lightning and thunder—and I didn't really see the light in the barn—or what I *thought* might have been a light—again. And the sound—well, that was probably either thunder, or an animal, or the wind blowing things around . . ."

"A light in the barn? Where was the noise?" Cade asked sharply.

Jan was startled at his intensity. "Oh, I think it was probably my imagination. I'm not used to living in the country, or familiar yet with all the sounds here. And besides, so much happens in the city that one becomes rather suspicious. . . ." Just then the children came running back with Tiger at their heels. "Please don't say anything to the children. I don't want them to tease me, or to be frightened because of my silly imagination."

Cade didn't ask any more questions, but when they turned to go, he walked along with them. Although he knew where they lived, he had not felt the time was right to stop by sooner. They all chatted, and the twins wanted to know if he'd caught any fish that day, which he hadn't. "Are you on vacation, Cade?" Tallie asked, and he told her he had a couple of weeks off and that someone had loaned him the cottage and boat. "Knowing how much I like to fish," he added.

He took Jan's hand to help her over a couple of awkwardly placed logs. He released her hand quickly, startled, and Jan wondered if he had felt the same jolt she had. *Maybe we're just AC and DC,* she thought, but the tingle spread throughout her body. He walked with them on up the hill and back to the house as they chatted about this and that. Tiger was back on the leash again and walked sedately between the twins. When they got back to the house, Jan grasped her courage in two hands and invited him in for coffee, or a cool drink. He smiled his acceptance. "Thanks, that sounds good. I've been out on the water for hours. I sort of lose sight of time out there."

They all trooped inside, and Trey unclipped the leash from Tiger, who took a long drink from his water bowl, then went to a corner of the big, sunny kitchen and plopped down on an area rug. "I think we tired him out, AnJan," Tallie worried.

"I'm sure he'll be all right," Jan replied as she got the pitcher of lemonade out of the refrigerator. "Dogs take more naps than humans do, you know." She reached for the cookie jar and put some cookies on a plate in the middle of the big, round oak table, while the twins were putting ice cubes in the glasses. They all sat down and enjoyed the chocolate chip cookies and lemonade.

"This is my favorite cookie," Cade remarked in his deep voice, with a slow smile at Jan.

Jan queried with amazement, "You mean there *is* some other kind of cookie?"

He flashed his startling white grin at her in appreciation. The pink of her T-shirt was flattering, despite her dark red hair, and her figure, he decided, was made for T-shirts.

With the twins chattering away, there was not much opportunity for him to ask any more questions about the previous night. He realized, too, that she could indeed have imagined the light and noise, but with his background he preferred not to take any chances.

"What are those other buildings back there?" he asked, gesturing toward the backyard. When they all answered by enumerating what buildings were there, all rather delapidated, he showed enough interest, without too much eagerness, that they offered to show him around.

They trooped out the back door, with Tiger waking up and eagerly following them out. They pointed out the well house with its covering of yellow roses, and the as yet uncleaned chicken house. "I'm leaving that for Char and Tom." Jan laughed. "I refuse to cope with poultry, let alone the dirt, droppings, and old feathers in there!"

She pointed out the old, long-untended orchard and the shallow pond, edged with cattails, out behind the barn. There was some fruit forming on quite a few of the trees, despite the obvious lack of care in recent years. The gnarled old apple and pear trees were showing a number of small, hard, green fruit, as were the plum trees. Even the cherry tree was showing little green fruits, no larger yet than the pits that would be their centers when ripe.

The old barn dominated the backyard. Unpainted for many years, there were spaces between many of the boards, and the entire building had a northward cant to it. Cade casually strolled in that direction. "Any stalls in the barn? Any hay?"

"I'm not sure what all is in there—it's dark."

"And spooky!" interjected Tallie.

". . . and full of spiderwebs!" continued Jan. "I don't 'do' spiders."

"Okay if I look around? I wonder if it could ever be used again. Or is your brother-in-law planning to just pull it down and put up a new building?"

"I'm not sure, really. It looks pretty crummy, but I'm no construction expert." She gestured. "Be my guest."

Tallie didn't want to go in, either, but Trey trailed along behind Cade. Jan knew he wouldn't have gone in alone, but with Cade and Tiger there, he bravely followed.

Cade made a quick survey of the building, noting things Trey—and others—might not have. When he came out, he looked grim, but no one noticed because Tiger had discovered a mouse and was chasing after it. He overran it, and the mouse escaped into the briars and eventually through a hole back into the barn. Tiger backed out of the briars, yelping in pain. Jan and the twins ran over to him and checked his nose and paws for thorns. "Reminds me of the thorn in the lion's paw," muttered Jan. "Maybe we should call him Aesop!"

Chapter Three

In spite of the twins' eager invitation to Cade to stay for dinner—"We're having hamburgers and potato salad!"— he politely (and, Jan hoped, reluctantly) refused, with a "Sorry, I can't do it tonight. Thanks anyway." He looked hopefully at Jan. "Perhaps another time?" he said as he headed toward the driveway, already in a departure mode. Jan smiled as she trailed along, listening to the twins chattering nonstop to Cade. Although she had not seconded the invitation, she wasn't sure he'd noticed. In spite of Cade's being one of the most intriguing—not to mention ruggedly attractive—men she had ever met, her teacher's caution reminded her that she really did not know anything about him. But how to find out? Ask Cheryl? *Well, I'll try her, although if he's just here for a couple weeks, it's unlikely. It won't hurt to ask!* She smiled to herself.

After their "delicious" dinner, Trey and Tallie took Tiger outside again to romp and play. Taking advantage of

the break, Jan called Cheryl Norris to see if she knew anything about Cade. Although Cheryl hadn't met him, she
knew the owner of his cottage and assured Jan that Mr.
Brooks wouldn't rent it to anyone unreliable or dangerous.
"They live just three doors away and would be very careful
on behalf of everyone in the area." Then she teased, "Is
he that handsome?"

"Well, I wouldn't say handsome, necessarily, but very
attractive in a rugged, outdoorsy way. Thanks for the re-
assurance. Perhaps"—Jan cleared her throat—"perhaps
we can get . . . better acquainted."

Cheryl chuckled. "If you need references, I'll be glad to
call Mr. Brooks."

"Yes, well, thanks. Cade doesn't seem too interested, or
he would have followed up sooner, I'd think. However . . ." She changed the subject. "By the way, I'm
thinking of taking Tallie and Trey to the aquarium in Seattle Thursday. Do you think Emily and Robby might like
to come along?"

"I'm sure they'd love to, but won't that be a lot of hassle
for you?"

"Oh, no—as you know, kids are usually less trouble if
they have a friend along. I'll take Char's van so there'll be
plenty of room. I just have a little Miata, not large enough
for five! How about if I pick them up at eight-thirty in the
morning? That should give us plenty of time to get to the
ferry."

"Sounds good. Let me check and see if they'd like to
go, although I'm sure they would. Why don't I call you
back in a few minutes?"

While waiting for the return call, Jan walked out into the
backyard to check the children. She told them what she had
in mind about the aquarium and taking their friends along,

and the kids were excited at the prospect. "Can't we go tomorrow instead?" begged Trey.

"No, I want Tiger to have several days with us here before we go off and leave him behind," Jan said, reminding them this was his first day with them. "We'd better let him get used to us and his new home before going off without him. Mrs. Sawley said he would be all right home alone, but I'd rather wait a few days. Okay?"

The children reluctantly assured Tiger they wouldn't go off without him yet, and that they would *always* return. They were delighted when Cheryl called to say Robby and Emily would go with them to the aquarium on Thursday. The trips to the beach had sharpened their interest in sea life, Jan noted, so this would be further education for them without their realizing it.

During the next couple of days, the twins spent several hours with Emily and Robby. They were all becoming good friends, which pleased Jan. She wrote another letter to Char and Tom, reciting the things they'd been doing. She also urged Tallie and Trey to write to their parents and agreed that pictures did count as part of the letter if it was something they mentioned first.

They gave Tiger a lot of loving attention, welcoming him as a member of the family. He lapped it up like ice cream and returned the affection with much tail-wagging and sloppy kisses. Jan worried what would happen when Char put out some of her collectibles on the occasional tables, as Tiger's tail tended to make a clean sweep of them. He was big enough that he could rest his chin on the big kitchen table. It seemed as often as Jan told him to get his chin off the table, the twins encouraged him to put it back on.

They agreed that the daily walk on the beach was one

of the best parts of living on Whidbey Island and usually came back laden with shells, rocks, and pieces of driftwood that caught their attention. Tiger never tired of chasing whatever they'd throw, and sometimes he came back with surprises that they *hadn't* thrown, such as dead fish, seaweed, empty cigarette packages, and other trash.

"This dog is not the least bit discriminating," Jan complained. He was also everyone's friend, a real marshmallow, although when he barked to announce someone's arrival, he certainly *sounded* ferocious, for which she was grateful.

The Wednesday before the trip to the aquarium was wet and blustery. Robby and Emily had come to visit, which made both Cheryl and Jan rejoice at the individual peace and quiet each then reveled in. The kids were good at entertaining themselves. From Trey's room came the sound of motors as the boys played with the cars and trucks. From Tallie's room came the soft murmur of girls playing with dolls and, later, tea sets, as Tallie came out to beg for "tea and cookies."

Jan was curled up in the big brown platform rocker. Because of the wet, gray day and the encroaching shrubbery and trees, she turned on the light to better read her book. Her conscience urged her to do some unpacking for Char, but she justified her "laziness" as her reward for all her hard work and substitute parenting. *Who knows when things will be this quiet again so I can read?* she thought as she sipped her peppermint tea. *This is really nice—quiet, warm, comfortable, and I don't need to think about dinner for a couple of hours. No wonder Char often looks frazzled. Taking care of a house and two kids is a big job—plus she also has a husband to find time for!*

She didn't see Cade come up the driveway, but he could

see her through the window, the light by which she was reading highlighting her red hair. The picture tugged at something deep inside him. What would it be like to come home to someone like Jan and a home in the country every day? *Forget it. You have other things to do—important things,* he reminded himself, and shrugged. He wasn't even sure why he was showing up here, except he'd been fighting the urge ever since he'd last seen Jan. He hesitated there in the driveway, as though to turn back, when Tiger, who was lying on the floor near Jan, lifted his head and woofed softly. The dog smoothly rose and went to the window, then barked as he saw someone outside.

Jan looked up, startled, and saw what Tiger saw, but her reaction was pleased. She arose and went to the front door. "Come on in, Cade," she invited. "What can we do for you?"

"Well—" He hesitated, then mounted the steps to the porch. "I was a little restless, and my fridge is getting full of fish. I thought perhaps you and the kids might like some more fresh fish." He held out a plastic-wrapped offering.

"Only if it's cleaned!" Jan laughed. "I had never cleaned a fish before, and you should have seen how I butchered the last one you gave us." She added hastily, "But it was truly delicious!"

Cade quirked a grin, his eyes dancing, "Yeah, this one is cleaned." Entering the living room, he looked around. "Where are the twins?"

"Shh—listen," said Jan, pointing toward the stairs.

Cade heard the motor sounds and grinned again. "Cars, huh?"

"Yes, Emily and Robby Norris from up the road are here playing with Tallie and Trey. A wonderful rainy-day break for both Cheryl Norris and me!" She took the fish from him and headed for the kitchen. "Coffee?" she asked over her shoulder.

"Sounds good," he answered, following her through the dining room into the big kitchen, his eyes admiring her trim figure. There were still some unpacked boxes in both rooms although the living room was fairly well settled. He nodded toward the boxes. "Saving something for your sister to do when she gets back?" he teased.

"Yes, I figure she shouldn't get off scot-free!"

"How do they like New Zealand?"

"Oh, they love it! They called the other night. Tom's having some good business results, and Char is enjoying looking around Auckland. They plan to do weekend things when they can and see as much of the country as possible. Tom's business contacts have been very gracious to them." She turned the heat on under the teakettle. "I hope you don't mind instant coffee. I'm a tea drinker myself and make very poor coffee."

"Sure, that's fine. I've had far worse than instant in my line of work."

"Oh, what's that?"

"Uh, I work for the government. . . . I'm based in the Jackson Federal Office Building downtown." He turned toward the fridge. "What's all this?"

"The kids' artwork and part of Char's magnet collection. Everyone she knows buys unusual magnets for her—bringing them back from wherever they go, here and abroad."

Cade chuckled as he read some of the magnets' comments. "Hey, some of these are pretty good. . . . 'Life is uncertain; eat dessert first.' 'Chocolate is my middle name.' Oh, and here's one from the Black Forest—a cuckoo clock?"

"Yes, it's amazing what different kinds of magnets there are, wherever you go."

Jan poured the coffee for Cade, tea for herself, and set out some raisin-oatmeal cookies. She was very aware of Cade. Indoors, he seemed much bigger than at the beach, very large in what was actually a very spacious room. Their fingers brushed as they both reached for a cookie, and Jan again felt a quiver shoot up her arm. His eyes became a darker shade of blue as they mirrored the surprise in hers. In spite of the sip of tea she had just swallowed, her mouth felt dry.

A soft *woof* from the back door broke the moment. Tiger, who had stayed outside when Cade arrived, wanted in. Jan crossed to the door and opened it. Tiger wagged his tail in appreciation, then shook his big body, scattering water droplets everywhere. "Oh, Tiger!" exclaimed Jan as she reached for an old towel they kept near the door for just this reason. "Hold still while I wipe you off!"

Cade cleared his throat. "How is he settling in?"

"Really quite well. The twins adore him!"

"Have you heard any more noises, or seen any more lights at night?"

"No, but I'm not positive I did anyway. I really hope I didn't. I'd like to think everything is safe here on the island."

"Probably reasonably so. It's building up a lot. My dad was stationed here with the Navy for several years when I was a kid. There are sure a lot more people here now, though."

"Oh, you're a native, too, hmm?"

"Well, I was born in San Diego, but as a Navy brat I got to live in a lot of places, including here. I always liked

Washington State and was glad when my work brought me here.''

They talked for an hour, about different parts of the country, sports, current events, books. On some things they agreed, and on others they didn't. They were both baseball fans but wondered if there would ever be a World Series for the Mariners, in spite of their good showing the previous year. They agreed that all professional sports had become just a business. ''About the time you become an enthusiastic fan of a team,'' Cade commented glumly, ''half the team become free agents and are gone the following year. Or the owners move them to another city! They seem to have forgotten that fan loyalty means being able to identify with basically the same players, year after year.''

Jan agreed. ''Every team we play has several of our old—usually good—players on them.

If we had all the good players we've let go . . .''

And on it went. Several cups of coffee and a dozen cookies later, Cade got up to leave. ''I didn't mean to take up so much of your time,'' he apologized.

''Oh, but I've enjoyed it,'' Jan objected. ''I love the kids dearly, but adult company is very welcome.'' *Oh, great,* she thought. *Be a little obvious, Jan!*

''So have I,'' he replied, with a warm smile that made her tummy do funny flips.

''W-would you like to stay for dinner? We're having salmon,'' she invited, tongue in cheek.

He flashed his wonderful grin. ''Sorry, I have something I have to do. Maybe another time.'' He picked up his windbreaker, then said hesitantly, ''Uh—Jan?'' She raised her eyebrows in query as he took a small card from his jacket pocket and held it out to her. ''I'm sure you're right about the sound you heard the other night, but here's my number in case you ever think you hear something unusual . . . or anything. Although I'm not there all the time—as you know, I like to fish." He gave another grin. "But I'm usually there at night. And there's an answering machine. . . ."

She was touched. "How nice of you," she said. "I'm sure there's nothing to worry about, but I appreciate the offer." The part about his usually being there at night sounded good—perhaps no other entanglements? She pursed her lips. "Perhaps the next time I see a scary movie?" she teased.

"No problem," he said, and then, in a deeper tone, "Indeed, it would be my pleasure." He lightly touched her hand just before he went out the door, and she felt that same flutter of the pulse as she watched him walk around the house and out the driveway, her eyes just a little dreamy. Maybe summer on Whidbey was going to be more interesting than she'd anticipated.

She repeated this comment when she talked to Phyllis, who called that evening.

"Ooh, do tell all!" urged Phyllis.

"There isn't much to tell, Phyll," Jan admitted. "I think he likes me okay, but whether it's anything more, I don't know. He seems to spend most of his time fishing, so I guess he's on vacation. You'd think, if he *is* interested, that he'd ask me out, or try to spend more time with me. . . ."

"You're rather closely chaperoned, you know," Phyll said dryly. "And there's no obvious baby-sitter available, since you just moved to the area."

"Oh, don't be so reasonable!" Jan complained, then changed the subject. "How's your romance with Roy coming along?"

"Well, I have to admit, he's doing okay. *Very* helpful."

"In what way?"

"Any way I ask!" Phyllis said smugly.

"That good, huh?"

"Well, not *that* good. He's been stopping by almost every evening to see if there's anything he can do to help, and we had a lovely afternoon Sunday by the pool. He's *very* good at applying sunscreen!"

"A very important trait in a man, I always say." Jan giggled.

"No, we have lots of fun together—he has a great sense of humor." She paused. "And . . . he's a really terrific kisser!"

"Ah-hah, tell me more!"

Their conversation extended for almost an hour, as they caught up not only on Roy but on other friends who had stopped by to see Phyllis. Phyll's mother had driven her to the doctor, and the leg was healing well. Phyllis was curious about the farm, and Jan invited her—and Roy, if she wished to invite him—to come out for the Fourth of July. "We'll have a picnic. We'll grill hamburgers, I can make potato salad, and other picnic-type stuff."

Phyll promised to call back the next evening with the answer. "But even if Roy can't make it, I'll come."

"You can't drive with a broken leg!" Jan protested.

"Sure I can. I've been driving around town some. But I'll try to get Roy to come. Just think how romantic the ferry ride back in the moonlight will be. . . ."

That night the rain muffled all sound of the movements that startled the night creatures. Tiger was warm and cozy in the house and had already learned to ignore the various noises made by the old house. Not only were the children snuggled all tight in their beds, but Jan, too, was asleep, dreaming delicious dreams of a certain tall, dark, handsome man.

Thursday morning dawned pink and clear, with just a few scattered white cloudlets floating in the azure sky. Everyone was bright and chipper, looking forward to the trip to the aquarium in Seattle. Jan had checked the ferry schedule but didn't worry overly since the summer schedule, one every half hour during the day, was in effect.

Dressed in casual clothes, which translated to jeans and T-shirts, they left Tiger in the garage with plenty of food and water. She was concerned enough about his reaction, however, to tiptoe back after the kids were in the car and she'd started the engine. Tiger was stretched out on his cedar bed, which Trey had carried there for him, and was already half asleep, obviously used to being left home alone.

They stopped at the Norris house to pick up Emily and Robby. An intense discussion ensued as to who would sit in the center seat of the van and who in the back one. Jan settled it by saying the girls would sit in the center going into Seattle, and the boys in the center seat coming back. At her urging, they had all brought a few small toys to while away the driving time, but when she pulled the car onto the ferry at Clinton and cut the engine, Jan said, "Topside, everyone! And no running!" they were all fast off the mark, heading for the bow deck.

The ferry was not as full as it would be during commuting hours or holiday weekends, such as the Fourth of July the following week. The loading process went forward in a very businesslike manner, and soon the ferry was tooting its departure warning. Jan and the children went out to the forward end of the ferry to enjoy both breeze and view.

The gray and white seagulls were screaming and diving around the ferry. There was an incredible view of both the Olympic Mountains to the west and the Cascade Mountains to the east. Both were still topped with snow, so bright in the sunshine as to be almost blinding. Ten-thousand-foot-tall Mount Baker towered above the surrounding peaks to the north, while much farther to the south fourteen-thousand-foot Mount Rainier dominated the skyline. The evergreen forests, mainly fir, cedar, and hemlock, draped the mountainsides, although clear-cut patches, the result of logging in previous years, were much in evidence. The fresh breeze was strong enough to cause small whitecaps here and there on the water of Puget Sound, which was alternately cobalt blue and celadon green. The sun shone brightly from a clear, cerulean sky.

A truly delightful day to be alive, thought Jan.

To the east, just leaving the Mukilteo dock, they saw a sister ferry departing for Clinton. It was not long before the ferries passed in the middle of Possession Sound. They waved at the passengers on the other ferry, and received friendly waves in return. The children chattered and dashed back and forth, calling forth numerous "Don't run!" reminders from Jan.

As they approached Mukilteo, Jan herded her charges down the stairs to the car deck, and they buckled their seat belts in preparation to drive off the ferry. They were waved off the boat by the crew and started up the long hill that would lead them to the interstate, thence into Seattle. With the rush hour over, traffic was not too bad. She parked the van near Stewart and Ninth in downtown Seattle, and, since they were in the free-ride zone for the Metro buses, caught one that would take them down to the waterfront.

The day was a complete success, helped in no small measure by the perfect weather. In addition to enjoying the variety of sea life in the aquarium, they also caught the film at the OmniDome, then walked along the waterfront. They enjoyed fish and chips at Ivar's for lunch, and the children were delighted with Ye Olde Curiosity Shoppe. As Jan headed the van north on I-5 to catch the ferry home, the children reviewed the highlights of the day. Jan smiled as she listened to what had made the biggest impact: For the boys it had been the mummy in the Olde Curiosity Shoppe; for the girls, the fragile, beautifully colored tropical fish at the aquarium.

Because they had spent longer playing tourist than she'd planned, they got caught in the evening commute, which meant going painfully slowly at times. Seattle reputedly had the sixth-worse commuter traffic in the country, and Jan was ready to believe it as they crawled along. As they turned off the interstate toward Mukilteo and the ferry, Jan said she was happy it wasn't Friday, when there'd be twice as much traffic! The ferry was almost full when they arrived, and it filled up before their turn came to board, so they settled down to a half hour's wait for the next ferry.

A tap on her door caught Jan's attention. She turned around from facing back toward the children, and standing there was Cade. She blinked and asked, "What are you doing here?"

"I might ask you the same." He smiled. "Where have you been?"

Before she could answer, the children eagerly detailed their day.

"Sounds like you've all had a busy day," he responded. "I have what I think is a first-class idea. Jan, how about I treat you all to dinner over at the restaurant?" He nodded toward the restaurant just north of the car/ferry holding area.

Her eyes brightened, but before she could acquiesce, the children were responding, "Yeah!" "All right!" "Please, AnJan!" "That sounds like fun!" "I'm starved!" "I can't wait to get *home* to eat!" "Please, can't we eat with Cade, AnJan?!"

"It sounds unanimous." Jan smiled at Cade. "Let me pull the car out of this line so I can park behind the restaurant."

"Okay, I'll go move mine, too. I was just going to pick up a sandwich until I saw you here." He gave her a warm look, his voice a low rumble. "Now a candlelit dinner sounds much better."

Despite herself, Jan blushed, then quickly nodded, replying, "See you in a couple of minutes." He waved as he turned toward his car, a satisfied smile on his face. What had been a difficult, frustrating day looked like it had taken a turn for *much* better, even with four kids along.

Fifteen minutes later, they were all together in the restaurant's entrance area, after Cade had taken the boys with him to the Fishermen's Restroom and Jan and the girls had used the Mermaids' Restroom. Jan had brushed her hair and freshened the lipstick that had long since worn off. Looking at her image in the mirror dubiously, she had opened her compact to see if she could subdue the effect of the sun and wind on her face.

After rejoining Cade and the boys, Jan excused herself for a few minutes to call Cheryl Norris to see if she had any objections to the children getting back a little later. Cheryl was very agreeable, saying that a peaceful dinner for just her and her husband, David, would be a rare treat. "See you later!"

"Any problem?" asked Cade. The children queried the same with their eyes.

"No problem at all." The children sighed in relief. Just then the hostess came to usher them to their table. Cade held Jan's chair for her, brushing his hands over her shoulders after pushing it in. He set the girls next to Jan and the boys next to himself, but made sure he was beside Jan at the round table. Jan looked at the prices and frowned. "Perhaps we'd better go Dutch," she suggested.

"No problem," Cade replied. "I picked up my paycheck today, and it's burning a hole in my pocket."

"But five extra mouths . . ."

"Please—I want to," he responded, putting his hand on hers, looking into her eyes. "I particularly like—" He paused. "—the company." He smiled warmly at her.

Jan looked into his deep blue eyes, almost drowning, feeling the warmth of his hand. His palm was rough, she supposed dreamily, from all the boating and fishing. Very stimulating, that roughness on her much smaller, softer hand. Her heartbeat quickened, and she breathlessly acceded to his request.

The waitress interrupted, "Can I get you anything to drink?"

Cade released Jan's hand reluctantly and turned to the children. "What would you like to drink? Coke? Pepsi? A Roy Rogers or Shirley Temple?" The named drinks carried the day. "How about you, Jan? A cocktail perhaps?"

"No, I don't think so, since I'm driving. Iced tea with lemon will be fine." She smiled softly at him, noticing as she did so the pupils of his eyes dilating.

Cade gave the drink order to the waitress, and then he and Jan discussed dinner options with the children. Having already had fish that day, the kids all opted for hamburgers.

Jan and Cade agreed they'd go for the mesquite-grilled salmon. Jan smiled at Cade. "You can never get too much salmon!"

While not a noisy affair, dinner was certainly not quiet. The children were still talking about what they had seen and done that day. Jan was amazed that despite the children's presence she was very conscious of Cade. Their arms occasionally brushed, as did their knees. Awareness intensified between them, in spite of their companions' chattering presence.

For dessert, the children asked for ice cream sundaes. Cade and Jan ordered the crème brûlée, which melted sensuously on their tongues. As Cade paid the bill, Jan gathered the children together and reminded them to thank Cade for the delicious dinner, which they did with enthusiasm.

Once on the ferry, the children sat down at one of the tables with the deck of cards Cade had extracted from his car's glove compartment, and he said firmly to them, "Sit. Play. Behave." They all nodded. Then he and Jan walked out on deck, finding a spot by the railing where they watched the sun descending low into the west. The ferry was heading straight into the sun's setting path. They leaned against the railing, and soon he put his arm casually across her shoulders. "Warm enough?"

"Mmm," she murmured, leaning into him. "It's so beautiful, isn't it?"

He pulled her closer and looked directly into her velvety brown eyes and answered in his low, rumbly voice, "Very." Leaning closer, he lightly kissed her ear. She closed her eyes as a tremor went through her.

"Are you sure you're not cold?" he asked as he drew her even closer.

"Mmm," she murmured again, her awareness of the

length and strength of his body felt in every fiber of her being. Her eyes fluttered open, and she gazed up at him.

Cade turned her toward him, his other arm going around Jan to pull her fully against him. "I'll be happy to keep you warm." He grinned. His right hand cupped her cheek, and she felt the roughness of his thumb brush back and forth across her lower lip. Sounds disappeared as they focused totally on each other. His lips hovered over her face, then gently touched her forehead . . . her cheek . . . her ear. . . .

Jan turned her face slightly into his, and their lips touched lightly, softly, brushing each other. Jan could feel the crackle of awareness between them. Closing her eyes, she saw sparklers and stars as the blood rushed through her body. Cade gathered her closer to him, his hand leaving her face and circling her waist, so their bodies clung, shoulder to shoulder. Jan's arms had somehow made their way around Cade, holding him closer to her.

The raucous sound of the ferry's horn startled them, but even then they were slow to pull apart. Jan glanced around, realizing there were other people there on the deck with them. She flushed a little. "It's not even dark. I . . . I . . ."

"That's okay—it doesn't have to be dark, does it?" He loosened his hold on her but continued to keep one arm around her shoulders, holding her close against his side. "But if you like, we'll try again after dark." He chuckled softly against her hair.

"Oh, well . . . I didn't mean . . ." Jan was not often flustered. She shrugged her shoulders. "Back to the sunset . . ."

Cade volunteered to take the boys with him in his Bronco, and followed Jan and the girls in the van, allowing a fair distance between the vehicles. The girls were so busy chattering that they didn't notice Jan's abstraction during the drive north on the island, although the farther they went the quieter the girls became, tired after a busy day.

As she drove, Jan wondered if Cade would stay for a while when they arrived home. As she recalled those few minutes in his arms, she was amazed at her reaction. She could not recall ever having been so lost to her surroundings as she had been there on the foredeck of the ferry. For some reason, her mind had always before continued operating clearly when in a clinch. There was something about his touch, about his warm, smoky voice that reached deep within her. *He makes my toes absolutely curl,* she thought.

In the Bronco, Cade was wondering the same thing. *You'd better watch it, buddy,* he thought. *You're right in the middle of a job, and you don't need complications. And Jan could definitely become a* big *complication! Better go straight home after dropping the boys,* he regretfully concluded. Life appeared to be tossing him a curve when he was totally involved in this current case and didn't have the time for much of a personal life. There was no telling how long this case would drag on, and it wouldn't be fair to Jan to start something and then perhaps have to leave. On the other hand . . .

When they reached the Norris home, Cheryl and David came out to meet them. Jan introduced Cade to them, and they all stood there chatting for a few minutes, before Jan and Cade drove on home with the twins.

Cade walked them to the garage, where they received a frenzied welcome from Tiger, and then to the back door. Tiger made a quick circuit of the yard, then followed the twins into the house. Turning to Cade, Jan inquired, "Coffee?"

"Thanks, but . . . no. I'd better head on down the hill."

His look was a mixture of regret and desire. Taking her chin in his hand, he pushed back the silken dark red hair, his blue eyes darkening as he gazed into her velvety brown ones. "Jan.... Ah, Jan!" Cade tipped up her face as he leaned toward her, lightly covering her lips with his. Her hands came up against his chest as his lips slid over her cheek, then returned to her soft, slightly parted lips.

"Cade . . ."

"AnJan! Can we have some ice cream? I'm starved!" Trey interrupted the moment as he came into the kitchen and toward the back door. Jan sprang away from Cade, who raised his eyebrows, allowing his eyes to twinkle ruefully at her. Jan blushed a little but was reminded that being in loco parentis did not necessarily extend to "smooching," as the children would describe it.

"Sorry, but . . ." She spread her hands in a gesture of "what can I do?"

"Maybe just as well, for now," he murmured as Tallie joined in the ice cream request. "I'll see you . . . soon." Then, he said, including the twins, "Good night, all. See you on the beach?"

"Yeah, sure!" "Thanks for dinner!" "That's a real cool car, Cade. Thanks for the ride!" "Watch out for Tiger!"

Jan had the last word as she watched him stride toward the Bronco. "Coward!" He didn't hear her, and she wasn't sure if she meant Cade or herself with that descriptor.

Friday, Jan and the twins decided it was time to plant a garden, and the discussion of what to plant extended breakfast an extra half hour. Jan's parents had always had a garden when she was growing up, but, as was typical, she had worked in it under duress much of the time.

"Let's start small and simple," she urged when the twins

cited a long list of vegetables they should have in their very first garden, a different reaction than several weeks earlier when Jan had first suggested it. "And we'll need some tools—spade, hoe, rake."

"Manure—don't forget manure!" Trey urged.

"Oh, ick, pee-yew!" exclaimed Tallie. "We don't want a smelly garden!"

"That's okay, Tallie," Jan interjected. "We can get some bags of cured manure at the store—as well as our seeds, of course, and some tomato plants."

"Let's go!" Trey was halfway to the door.

"Whoa, wait a minute. Let's take a look in the garage and see what tools are already here. There's no point in buying anything we don't need."

Tallie said, "I think we've got some, 'cause Mom and Dad always had flowers 'n' stuff. Maybe they're behind the lawn mower?"

"Good thinking, Tallie," praised Jan. "Let's go look." The twins were out the door in a flash and found that the Trehearnes' gardening tools were, indeed, sitting in a back corner behind the mower and some other tools.

"Good," Jan remarked with satisfaction. "Let me get my purse and keys, and we'll go into town to get some seeds and stuff." She added, "Everyone brushes teeth first, however—and there are breakfast dishes . . ."

Tallie and Trey were already racing into the house to see who could reach the bathroom sink first for the teeth brushing. Jan laughed to herself and went only as far as the kitchen, where she cleared the table, put away the milk, and rinsed the dishes in the sink. No reason why they wouldn't keep until the dinner dishes were added. Maybe a stop at McDonald's was in the cards for lunch . . .

With Tiger in the back of the van, they set off. At the

seed and feed store, they were all inclined to get carried away. They bought seeds for beans, lettuce, radishes, peas (despite the fact that it was really too late in the season), and carrots, plus tomato and pepper plants, some onion sets, and even a few seed potatoes. They also purchased three bags of cured steer manure and two bags of organic compost, all tossed in the back of the van with Tiger, and gardening gloves for Jan and Tallie. She purchased a few extra pairs, "just in case." She'd already noticed Tiger had a tendency to pick up stuff in his mouth and not always return it to the same place. Jan then insisted they stop at the library afterward to pick up a few gardening books. "I know we'll all have some questions." While there, all three of them chose some books for reading. Jan noticed that Trey picked up a Hardy Boys book, and one of Tallie's books was a Nancy Drew mystery. *Some things never change,* she thought.

"Can't we just call Grandma and Grandpa and ask them about gardening?" queried Trey.

"Well, yes, but we'll have lots of questions as we go along, and we don't want to bother them too often," Jan replied. "Just think, this will be an adventure—a gardening adventure—for us. When you go back to school this fall, you can tell your new friends about starting your first vegetable garden!"

Then they made a quick stop at McDonald's, so they were ready to start gardening when they reached home. By the end of the day, they were all tired and dirty. They had not taken into consideration that the grass and weeds would be so compacted and thus quite difficult to dig through, so their progress was slow, even with Tiger's enthusiastic assistance. One of the gardening books had instructions for planting potatoes in a garbage can with about ten inches of dirt in the bottom, then adding compost as the plants grew. You continued adding compost periodically until the container was full. The writer gave assurance that all they'd have to do would be reach down into the container and pluck up the potatoes as they matured. Trey was all for using one of their thirty-two-gallon plastic trash cans for this and had a knife all ready to cut the necessary holes in its bottom until Jan stopped him. Not only did she not want him using a knife in what could be a hazardous task, but she was all for getting a smaller-sized container to start with. That was added to the running list tacked to the kitchen bulletin board for the next trip to town.

When they trooped into the kitchen about five o'clock, Jan fixed lemonade for them all. "I'll tell you what, kids, you relax for a few minutes with the lemonade, and I'll run up and have a quick shower. Then I'll come down and fix dinner while you clean up."

Tallie and Trey were more than ready to lean back in the comfortably cushioned captains' chairs. They turned on the small kitchen TV to watch one of their favorite programs and thirstily drank their lemonade. Trey found a bag of potato chips for them to nibble on. Tiger flopped down beside them, his eyes alert for any dropped crumbs.

When Jan came down, hair still damp, she commented, "Oh, I feel so much better! Don't you want to get showers now?" Trey was too comfortable to move, but Tallie decided she felt too "icky" and would have a shower, too.

Dinner was quick and easy—hot dogs with all the accoutrements, the remaining potato chips, tossed salad, applesauce, and chocolate chip cookies. The children chattered about their day, showing pride in their accomplishments. "How long will it be until we can eat some stuff, AnJan?" Trey inquired.

"Ohh . . . three weeks, at least, I think, before the onions and radishes are ready. And the lettuce says it takes forty-five days, so that would be early August. Of course, the weather is nice and warm, so maybe things will come along faster."

Trey and Tallie both thought that was "forever" away, but agreed that it would be fun to pick their own ripe veggies. They all pitched in on the dishes, with Jan washing, Tallie drying, and Trey putting away the dishes.

"Shall we take a walk down to the beach with Tiger and watch the sunset?" Jan asked.

"Yeah!" "Sounds good!" "How about that, Tiger, want to take a walk?" "Maybe we'll see Cade down there."

"Well, that's a possibility, isn't it?" Jan agreed, as though it had not occurred to her. "Grab a sweater or jacket; it's getting cooler out." She tucked a plastic bag in her jeans pocket, as someone always found something on the beach they *had* to bring back to the house.

Trey put Tiger on the leash for the walk down to the beach, and Jan locked the door behind them. The day had been beautiful, boasting a lovely blue sky with just a few puffy white clouds, and the temperature, at seventy-eight degrees, had been very comfortable—one of the best things about western Washington: Mild summers and mild winters!

As usual, the view across the water to the Olympic Peninsula and the Strait, was breathtaking. Mount Olympus, the highest of the Olympic Range, was still capped with snow. Although they couldn't see the Cascades from where they were located on the island, the mountains they could see were more than satisfactory. There were some sailboats out on the water, dipping and gliding before the wind.

South of them they could see the state ferry making the Keystone-to–Port Townsend run. There were a number of motor craft about, and a freighter was making for the Strait of Juan de Fuca on its way to the open Pacific.

Jan always enjoyed the beach. *It's so peaceful—it's as though the water washes any worries or aggravations away,* she thought. The children romped up and down the beach with Tiger, all of them enjoying the freedom and the warmth of the late-afternoon sun. These were the longest days of the year. Sundown came after nine o'clock, with twilight lingering until ten or after. Jan perched on one of the driftwood logs, well back from the water, and watched the children, glad they'd been able to get Tiger. He seemed to enjoy the children as much as they did him.

She was sitting with her knees pulled up close to her chin, her arms wrapped around them, unaware of Cade's approach until he leaned over and kissed the nape of her neck. She would have fallen off the log in surprise if he hadn't grabbed her shoulders. "Whoa, there!"

"Oh! You startled me!" The blood raced through her body, and her breath caught in her throat as she looked up at him, sharply aware of his very masculine attraction. His dark hair was ruffled by the breeze, and the royal blue shirt he wore caused his eyes to appear a deeper blue than usual.

"Sorry." He sat down next to her on the log and leaned toward her. "Mmm, you smell wonderful. What *is* that scent you wear? Some kind of flower?"

She smiled, almost *too* pleased to see him. "Honey-suckle."

"I knew there was a reason to call you honey." He grinned. "How are you and"—he nodded toward the twins—"the little terrors?"

She grinned back. "Oh, not too bad. Today we started

a garden.'' She inspected her hands, which, in spite of the gloves she'd worn, were the worse for wear, including a blister on her right thumb.

He looked at her hands too. He took her right one in his left hand, lifted it to his mouth, and gently kissed the thumb. Then he turned her hand palm up and kissed it slowly. Their eyes met, hers widening at the warm brush of Cade's lips on her palm. Her other hand clenched at her side as he kissed her palm again, softly, warmly. ''Better?'' he murmured.

''Oh, much!'' she said breathlessly. ''Uh . . .'' She cleared her throat. ''How was your day? Did you, uh, catch anything?''

Reminded of his long vigil, he sighed. ''No, nothing today, I'm afraid,'' he said, although his reference was not to fish.

''Too bad.'' She sighed again as she looked out over the water. ''Isn't this absolutely beautiful? I wish I could live by the water. It just seems to wash all stress away.''

''Well, yes, it can do that, can't it?'' he replied. ''I guess I, umm, concentrate so hard . . . on catching fish, that I don't always notice, but I do enjoy the peace and quiet.'' Then he added, ''But the water can be very dangerous, too.''

''That's true,'' Jan agreed. ''Water, wind, fire—all of them can be both good and bad, can't they?''

Cade nodded as his eyes ranged over the view before them, observing the boats' directions and activities. ''Those terrible floods in the Midwest a few years ago, and the floods here last winter!''

Cade did not release Jan's hand as they sat there, enjoying their intermittent discussions and the silences. They leaned against each other, chuckling quietly at the antics of the children, dog, and seagulls. The children would toss pebbles into the air. Both Tiger and the gulls would pursue, with the gulls screeching their anger when they discovered the duplicity.

The sun continued its westward journey, casting long shadows as it moved closer to the horizon. The trees behind them swayed gently in the light breeze. The twins came up to them from time to time, happy to see Cade, then off they'd troop, laughing and chattering.

"How sad that not everyone can enjoy such peace as this," Jan commented.

Cade's hand gripped hers tightly. "Yeah, there are a lot of folks all over who don't know what it's like," he said grimly. "And sometimes things aren't as peaceful as they seem on the surface."

"What do you mean?" she asked quickly.

He caught himself. "Well, for instance, under that water is the food chain, from krill all the way up to whales, one eating the other." He didn't bring up the ultimate villain—man.

She shuddered. "I think I like my view better."

"So do I—but we can't ignore that the other is there."

Jan looked at Cade questioningly, surprised at his somber tone of voice. He looked back at her. "Sorry, I didn't mean to sound so grim. Look there." He nodded again to the west, where the sun was dropping closer to the horizon, starting to emanate its setting colors. He put his arm around her shoulders, pulling her against him. She felt just right there, close and warm and fragrant.

The twins came up, tired from their running and playing. Tallie sat on the other side of Jan, who put her arm around her, and Trey dropped to the sand in front of them, next to Tiger.

Cade thought to himself, *Anyone looking at us would think we're a family.* He felt a deep twist of longing within him, but banished it quickly. *Now, none of that! Remember, you're the original love 'em and leave 'em, never-make-commitments man. Besides, you've got a job to do. You can't let them get in the way—or* be *in the way. They might get hurt!* He stared west blindly, concentrating on getting himself in hand.

Jan continued to lean against Cade, rubbing her left hand up and down Tallie's arm. The colors of sunset flared and spread, pink and rose and salmon, lavender and mauve, orange and scarlet—a symphony for the eyes. But even as they oohed and ahhed, the orange disk slipped beyond the horizon. Jan sighed. "Words cannot describe that," she murmured.

"Oh, AnJan, that was *so* pretty!" Tallie chirruped.

Jan hugged her. "Yes, it was. But you know what else it was? That was the signal for bedtime!"

"Aw, AnJan!" Trey objected. "It's still early."

"It's after nine, dear, and we've all had a long day. Remember all that hard work we did?"

"I'll walk you home," Cade volunteered. "You shouldn't be out here alone this late."

"You think someone might come up behind me—" She watched the children, trudging up the hill ahead of them with Tiger. "—and . . . kiss me on the neck?"

"Hey, next time it might be Count Dracula!"

Their shared laughter reached softly into the twilight, and Jan recalled it with a smile as she snuggled into her bed later. *What a lovely way for the day to end,* she thought as she drifted off to sleep.

Chapter Four

Everyone moaned and groaned the next day about the aches and pains left from their gardening. "But we're not done yet," Jan pointed out.

"Aw, AnJan," grumbled Trey, "look at all we planted yesterday! Isn't that enough?"

"But look at all the seeds we have left. I know it's hard work, but . . ." She paused. "Well, I suppose we could take today off and then go back at it tomorrow. I guess another day won't make much difference."

The phone rang, and Tallie rushed to answer it. Apparently it was Emily, and Jan turned back to her second cup of tea and the morning paper, not paying attention to the phone conversation. Suddenly, Tallie was jumping up and down, "Oh AnJan, can we go horseback riding at Emily's? Please, please, please, please, *please?* Emily says it's okay with her folks if Trey and I come over. Please, can we, huh? I've always wanted to go horseback riding! And Slap and Happy are *very* tame! Please can we, please!''

''Whoa, slow down there, pardner—pardners,'' Jan added as Trey added his enthusiastic seconds. ''Well, I suppose it would be okay. Let me talk to her mother, though.''

''That's not necessary—just yes or no!'' Tallie pointed out. ''She's already asked her mom.''

''I'm sure it's okay, but I still want to talk to Cheryl, honey,'' she repeated. Tallie repeated the request on the phone, then held it out to Jan.

''Hi, Cheryl? Are you sure you want to take on these kids? As far as I know, the only riding they've done is ponies at the fair.''

''No problem, Jan. The horses are very gentle, and David and I will be out there with them. We have hard hats for them to wear, too.''

''How about boots?''

''Oh, their Nikes will be fine. Be sure they're wearing jeans, though, not shorts.''

''Okay, if you're sure. I'll send them on along.''

''Great. Oh—and if you don't mind, they can stay for lunch, too.''

''That's fine—and I appreciate it! See you later.'' She turned to the twins. ''Okay, you can go.'' She noticed they were already in jeans and had on their Nikes. ''You listen to Mr. and Mrs. Norris, and be sure to say please and thank you. They've invited you for lunch, too—don't forget your manners.''

''Aw, AnJan, you sound just like Mom!'' Trey protested.

''Maybe that's because we're sisters, and this is the spiel we used to get from *our* mom!'' She grinned at them. ''Go along and have a nice time. Maybe I'll work in the garden on my own.''

She kept Tiger in the kitchen with her and through the window watched them dash across the open field, with a few scattered firs, between their and the Norris property and saw Emily and Robby run to meet them. *I'm so glad for such nice next-door neighbors, and especially that there are children for Trey and Tallie to play with. That means so much to kids. And I'm sure Char and Cheryl will hit it off. Now, what shall I do? An entire free morning to myself! Read? Garden? Go shopping?*

She wandered out the back door, a fresh cup of tea in one hand, the other on Tiger's collar so he wouldn't dash after the twins. She viewed the previous day's gardening attempts with wry humor. *I wonder what Dad will say when he sees this,* she wondered, remembering the straight rows in her parents' garden in past years. The rows Jan and the twins had made in their garden were crooked. *Oh, well, as I recall, by midsummer the plants were always so big and sprawling we couldn't tell if we had started with straight or crooked rows!*

"Well, Tiger, what do you think?" she asked. "Do you think anything will grow?" Tiger gave a mild *woof* in reply. Jan strolled around the yard, leaning closer to smell the honeysuckle and roses, reaching down here and there to pull a weed. Although she loved the twins dearly, it was nice to have some peace and quiet to enjoy the country. The robins were singing happily, and the swallows darted and swooped for insects to take to their babies. They were nesting under the eaves of the barn, she noted, and recalled that swallows often returned year after year to use the same nest. She wondered how many years they had been returning to this old barn.

Wandering in that direction, she again thought about how nice it would be to live out in the country all the time. Her next thought, oddly enough, was of Cade. He was so good-looking—not handsome good-looking, but virile and manly and rugged. *He has that certain something—at least for me! Those blue eyes . . . and that deep voice! I wonder if he lives in Seattle? Or maybe he's going to rent that house indefinitely, not just for a couple weeks or for the summer. Of course, if he lived in Seattle—or Bellevue—I could see him more easily after Char and Tom get back. Hmmm . . .*

Jan idly watched Tiger range to and fro, pausing to sniff here, rolling in the grass there. She was pleased that he had settled in so well with them and hoped Char and Tom wouldn't be too upset about her getting them such a large dog. There'd be no getting rid of him, as he and the twins had bonded. He'd decided to spend half the night in Tallie's room, then would move into Trey's room.

Tiger took off, nose to the ground. "I hope that's a rabbit you're chasing and not a mouse or rat," she commented aloud. Tiger scratched at the barn door, trying to get in. "Oh, come on, Tiger, you don't want to go in there. It's dirty and cobwebby, and not very pleasant." Tiger, however, persisted, scratching and whimpering, until she threw up her hands, the remainder of her tea sloshing out of the cup, and said, "Oh, all right." She walked over to the door and unlatched and opened it. "There, you see? Just as I told you. Dirt and cobwebs and some musty old hay!"

Tiger raced back and forth, nose to the floor, whuffing and sniffing. Jan turned away, strolling back toward the house. Let the dog have his fun and games. *I'll go back later and close the door. Who knows, perhaps he'll kill some mice or rats—or at least chase them away!*

Entering the kitchen, she collected the breakfast dishes

from the table and carried them to the sink. It didn't take long to wash them and place them in the rack to drain. She swept the kitchen floor, transferred some laundry she'd started before breakfast from the washer to the dryer, started another load of laundry, then did some tidying in the living room.

With the washer and dryer rumbling off in the distance, she picked up the paper from the previous day to put it in the used paper rack in the kitchen. A headline caught her eye, and she turned the paper over to the start of the piece. It was about the drug traffic that not only plagued the entire world but apparently was fairly active in Island County. Since Whidbey Island was placed quite strategically close to Canada and the shipping lanes, it was suspected that drugs were coming ashore in some quantity. The sheriff's office was asking people to report anything suspicious they observed. He warned the public not to take matters into their own hands. Any tips were welcome, and one's name need not be given; but if it was, confidentiality was promised.

Jan sat down abruptly on a kitchen chair. *Wow! I never thought about that happening—the island is so peaceful and quiet. But I suppose it does make sense, being surrounded by water and all. I remember reading a few years ago that there were rumrunners in this area back in the thirties, during Prohibition.*

Just then the dryer beeped its "I'm done" sound, and she went into the laundry room to take out the dry clothes. The washer had completed its cycle as well, so she transferred its load to the dryer and started it up again, then took the dry clothes to the kitchen table to fold. She turned on the radio for some easy-listening music and sang along with Natalie Cole.

As she folded clothes, she thought about the newspaper article she had just read. Having lived in the metropolitan Seattle area most of her life, she had not only heard about drugs but had had them offered to her when she was in school. She had always refused them, but she had been more strongly reminded of their harm since she'd been a teacher, working with teenagers. If she had the power, she would eradicate them completely from the world, except for the limited use of some of them for medical needs.

I don't know why I'm so surprised that they bring drugs into Whidbey Island—with all this water, the authorities can't watch everywhere at once. I must say, I'm glad we're not living right on the beach.

She'd forgotten that Tiger was still roaming around outside until she heard him barking out front. She went to look out the front window and saw a dusty blue pickup in the driveway. "I wonder who that is," she murmured, and went out on the front porch to see. A rather scraggly looking man in his thirties was eyeing Tiger, but stayed in the truck. "Will he bite?" he asked.

"Not if I tell him not to," Jan replied. No point in letting a stranger know what a marshmallow Tiger really was. "What do you want?"

"I, uh, heard that you might want a new roof on the house and, uh, barn," he replied, gesturing at the two buildings. "Looks like they need some fixin' up."

Tom and Char hadn't said anything about new roofs to Jan, so she merely answered, "Perhaps later."

"Uh, I'd be glad to take a look and submit a bid for the work. Wouldn't cost ya anything," he hastened to assure her.

"What company do you represent?" she queried him.

"Uh, well, uh—I do independent contracting," he re-

plied. He took off the Mariners' baseball cap he was wearing backwards on his head and swiped his liberally tattooed
arm across his forhead, then replaced the cap.

"Well, we'd need references. Do you have a folder or
pamphlet about your company that you can leave with me?
And your phone number?" She still had a hand on Tiger's
collar, and the man had cautiously remained in his truck.
"What is your name and your company's name?"

"Well, uh, I'm Johnnie Rollins. I, uh, don't have any
papers with me. But I do real good work, Miss," he assured
her.

Jan was less than impressed with the scruffy-looking
man and knew she would not feel comfortable with him
around her—or, for that matter, later around her sister or
the twins. "I'm not interested right now, thank you."

"Why don't I just take a look around anyway? I'll make
you a real good price," he urged.

"No thank you," she replied firmly. "We're not interested at this time." She turned away, keeping her hand on
Tiger's collar in a rather obvious way.

The man muttered what sounded like offensive words
under his breath, rammed the truck into reverse, and backed
out of the driveway faster than advisable, almost hitting a
passing car as he did so.

"Well, he certainly wasn't very pleasant, was he,
Tiger?" she said to the dog, releasing her hold on his collar. *Does someone like that really think I'd hire him just
out of the blue?* she thought. *After all, I have read about
the 'nightmare roofers' who hit South Florida after Hur-
ricane Andrew, as well as other wild stories. If he is legit-
imate, I'm sure he or someone from his company will be
back. More likely, however,* she added, stroking Tiger's
head, *he's one of those migrant repairmen who just goes*

around trying to bilk old people and women on their own.
She and Tiger walked back into the house. "I hope he got
the message about what a mean dog you could be! I
wouldn't want him wandering around here!" A thought
struck her. "You don't suppose he was trying to case the
place with an eye to burglary, do you?" she again queried
the dog. "I wonder if he's stopping at many other places
in the area?"

As they walked through to the kitchen, the dryer beeped
again, so she got that load of clothing and folded it, then
took it upstairs with her. Looking at the clock, she debated
whether to go shopping or work in the garden in the time
she had left before the twins came home, and opted for
gardening. *Once I'm back in the city, I'll wish I'd taken
more advantage of the sunshine and fresh air here,* she
thought as she retrieved tools, seeds, and wheelbarrow from
the garage. She put on her now quite soiled gardening
gloves and prepared to take up some more chunks of the
thickly matted grass.

She hummed as she worked, forgetting about the itiner-
ant roofer's visit, now and again tossing a stick for Tiger
to chase. She noted two of the cedars in the yard were at
a good distance from each other to support a hammock.
*Maybe I'll get the family a hammock as a housewarming
gift,* she thought. *A rest in a hammock sounds pretty good
about right now. Why am I doing all this hard work, when
it isn't even my garden, anyway?* But she continued, enjoying the warm sun and cool breeze, catching a whiff from
time to time of rose and honeysuckle. The bees were happily busy among the flowers, and from time to time a tiny
hummingbird would dip into the honeysuckle flowers.

Her mind shifted to Cade. She wondered why it was that
just a look or a touch on the hand from one man could
carry such impact, yet with another man it was so ho-hum.

She wished she knew more about him. What she had seen and learned, she liked—a lot. *Better be careful, Janetta,* she told herself. *This man could be dangerous to your emotional health!* But oh, he was attractive! Those intent blue eyes, that firm mouth, that deep, masculine voice, that muscular body . . .

Tiger came prancing over to her, his head held high and proud, to lay a gift at her feet. She screamed and jumped back. A mouse! He'd caught a mouse and brought it to her. And it was still alive. "Eek!" she cried, one part of her brain looking on and saying, *Eek? That's straight from the cartoons! Get real, girl!* She backed away hastily, and Tiger picked up the poor little mouse again and brought it over to her. "No, Tiger! Drop it!" Crestfallen, he again put the mouse down. The mouse lay there for a few minutes, then stirred. Tiger watched it, his ears perked, his head cocked to the side, ready to grab it again. "No, Tiger!" She grabbed his collar and led him to the house. "I realize you think you're doing something good, but if you have to go mouse hunting, please dispose of them far away from me. In theory I don't mind the idea of dead mice, but in person, he's such a cute little fellow. . . ."

Closing the back screen door, Jan got a dog bone for Tiger. "Yes, you're a good dog," she assured him. "I'm only glad there aren't snakes on the island for you to bring to me! *That* I couldn't forgive."

Glancing at the clock, she decided to have some lunch, and fixed a sandwich and iced tea and took them out to the front porch with her. Setting them on a small table next to the porch swing, she swung her feet up on the cushioned seat after giving herself a push to start the swing moving. Giving a big sigh, she said to an alert Tiger, "Now *this* is the life!"

By the time the twins got home in the late afternoon, Jan had quite a bit more garden prepared to receive the seeds they had left, but she had given up about four o'clock and gone into the house and had a refreshing shower.

"AnJan, AnJan!" they called out to her as they came in from the field. "AnJan, the Norrises have invited us to go to the races with them tonight. Can we please? Please, can we?"

"And I'm glad to see you, too. How was the horseback riding?"

"Oh, it was *wonderful,* AnJan," Tallie said ecstatically. "Slap and Happy are be-u-tiful horses, and so tame and nice! I want a horse, too. I'm going to write to Mom and Dad and ask them if I can have a horse, just like Happy!"

"Yeah, it was great," Trey said, then added, "But tonight they're going to the sprint car races over at Alger, and they invited us along. Can we go, huh, can we?"

"You mean you still have energy to spare?"

"Yeah!" "Of course!" "Can we go, please?"

"What kind of racing? And where exactly is Alger? How much does it cost and when is it over?"

"AnJan, you sound just like Mom," Tallie pointed out again.

"It's over near Burlington," said Trey. "It's a dirt track, and they go really fast! They have accidents and stuff . . ."

"That doesn't sound very nice."

"But no one gets hurt! Anyway, Robby says they've got a friend who races over there, and maybe we can go down and look at his car after the race! Please, can't we? Huh? *Please?*"

The phone rang just then, and Jan picked it up. "Hello?"

"Hi, Jan, this is Cheryl. Have the kids gotten home yet?"

"Yes, I think they must have run all the way. They're certainly excited! What's this about the races?"

"Well, David has a friend who races sprint cars there, and we usually go several times each summer. The kids have a blast, and we'd be glad to take Trey and Tallie with us."

"I should think you had enough of them already today," Jan joked, winking and smiling at the twins.

"Oh, no—they were very good, no problem at all. And as you recently pointed out to me," Cheryl said archly, "they do entertain one another!"

Jan laughed at hearing her owns words quoted back at her. "How much do the races cost? And what time would you be leaving—and getting home?"

"We'd leave about six o'clock. They run qualifying races before the finals, and have two different sized cars. We probably wouldn't get home before midnight or one o'clock, though. If they have a lot of pileups, the races can last quite a while."

"Well, if you're sure you want them . . . all right. How much is it so I can send the money along with them? Okay. Sure. Yes, I'll get them cleaned up and feed them. You'll pick them up here at six-fifteen? Fine . . ." The twins ran whooping up the stairs to start getting ready. "Thanks a lot, Cheryl. They seem to be really excited about going. Okay, see you later."

Jan hung up the phone, then called up the stairs to the twins. "Each of you be sure to take a shower before dinner. I noticed you smelled pretty horsey!" Then she went to the kitchen to fix the twins a quick meal. While the favored macaroni and cheese was cooking, she got her purse and took out enough money for admission to the races and for some goodies during the evening.

When the Norrises' car pulled into the driveway, Trey went racing out to the car, but Tallie lingered a few minutes. "You don't mind being alone, do you, AnJan? I *could* stay home with you if you'll be lonely."

Knowing how much Tallie wanted to go to the races, Jan hugged her niece and assured her she'd be fine. "You go and have a great time!" she said, and walked out to the car with her. She exchanged greetings with Cheryl, David, and the children, reminded the twins to behave and mind Mr. and Mrs. Norris, and wished them a fun evening.

She stood there and waved as they left, Tiger sitting beside her. "Well, Tiger, I guess it's just you and I tonight! I wonder if there's anything good on TV. Or"—she had a sudden thought—"I could drive in and see Phyllis for a few hours. Let's go call her." She trotted into the house and straight to the telephone. No answer. "Well, I'll wait a while and call again. I'll fix myself a glass of iced tea in the meantime." She looked at the macaroni and stirred it a little, debating whether to have some for dinner, then curled her lip at the gelatinous mess. She sat down at the table with her tea, then tried her friend again. Still no answer.

"Maybe she's out with Roy tonight—or at her folks' place," she observed to Tiger, then mocked herself. *Look at me, talking to the dog the way I've been doing today!* She dumped the macaroni mess in the garbage, then tried calling Phyll again. "Well, maybe it *is* just you and I tonight, Tiger," she said.

It occurred to her that she could take a walk down to the beach by herself—well, with Tiger. Perhaps Cade might be around? *Well, you* do *have his phone number, silly. This* is *the nineties! You could call him and invite him over. But to what? An exciting evening of TV viewing? Or will he think I'm offering much more than that? I don't want him getting the wrong idea . . . Well, we could play Scrabble or cards . . . Get real!*

Jan wandered into the living room aimlessly. She plumped some pillows, straightened a picture, and rearranged some whatnots on an end table. She knew she'd like to spend more time with Cade, knew that she was very attracted to him. If she had gotten acquainted with some other people on the island, she could invite one or two other couples over, and they could all play cards.

She continued to dither for a while, then shook herself. "This is dumb! Tiger, let's take a walk down to the water. Then maybe we'll drive into town and pick up a hamburger or a pizza." She got his leash, locked the back door behind them, and headed for the beach. The beautiful summer day was softly waning into a mellow evening, and the swallows were dipping and darting about in order to get enough insects to hold their babies over till morning. The frogs were starting to make their ribbiting presence known. Overhead, Navy jets made their noisy way home to NAS Whidbey Island at the north end of the island. She paused to look up at them, thrilled as always at their thunder. "I wonder, Tiger, if the Blue Angels will be performing here this summer? I'll have to check into that. They are *so* exciting to watch!"

Jan and the Great Dane strolled on down the gravel road to the beach. There were several other individuals and couples around, and from some of the homes nearby came the scent of meat barbecuing. The laughter and chatter hung on the still air as she and Tiger walked along the beach. With so many people around, she hesitated to turn him loose. Even though *she* knew he wasn't dangerous, others couldn't be sure.

"Jan!" She heard a voice calling her name and turned, her heart instantly thundering at the sound of that husky voice. There was Cade walking toward her, tall and tanned and smiling at her. "Oh, be still my heart," she murmured, then gave a welcoming smile as they walked toward each other. He looked around. "Where are the twins?"

"They've gone to the races with the Norrises," she replied. "Trey could hardly wait! I suspect I'm going to be hearing some increase in motor noises tomorrow."

"Have you had dinner yet?" he asked as he leaned over to pet Tiger.

"Are you asking Tiger or me?"

He grinned at her. "You, of course."

"Well, no; we were going to eat when we went back up to the house. I fixed macaroni and cheese for the twins before they left. It's one of their favorites, but I just couldn't face it."

"Neither have I. I wondered—would you like to go somewhere, since you're free for the evening? Maybe dinner at Maud's Mansion in Coupeville?"

"Maud's Mansion? What's that?"

"It's one of those old Victorian houses that's been transformed into a small hotel. They serve meals and drinks, and even have a small dance floor operating on Saturday nights."

"Well . . ."

"Oh, and they have great desserts! *Chocolate* desserts," he teased her.

"Oh, well then, how can I say no? I'll take Tiger home

and I'll change into something a little dressier," she said, gesturing at her jeans and T-shirt.

"Fine! I'll go clean up and get the car. Pick you up in—" He looked at his watch. "—forty-five minutes?"

"Great!" Jan sparkled at him. "Come on, Tiger. See you later, Cade," she tossed back over her shoulder as she and Tiger headed for the road.

Chapter Five

As Jan urged Tiger along, ignoring his desire to sniff every other plant along the road, she considered what to wear. She obviously hadn't brought her full wardrobe with her, and although she had not thought about meeting—and wanting to impress—someone special, she had tossed in some skirts, blouses, and a couple of summer dresses. Cade had not seen her yet in a dress, and she wasn't sure she wanted to "knock his socks off." "Who am I kidding, Tiger? Of *course* I want to knock his socks off!"

She decided on a summery white-printed pale aqua dress with spaghetti straps and a swirling skirt, and a white cardigan to drape around her shoulders. She carefully applied her light makeup and her signature honeysuckle scent. Then she slipped her nylon-clad feet into white, high-heeled shoes that emphasized her slender legs, which she considered one of her better features. She was glad that Cade was so tall. She really felt quite diminutive next to him.

Arriving exactly forty-five minutes later, Cade, too, had changed. In fawn slacks, white shirt, navy-and-red-striped tie, and navy blazer, he quite took her breath away. His blue gaze swept over her swiftly, with a warm glint of appreciation, and he said, "*Very* pretty—you look good enough to eat!" He leaned over and kissed her lightly on the cheek, inhaling her delicate scent. "And you smell honey-sweet. Mmm . . ."

Putting his arm around her shoulders, he led her out the front door, carefully locking it behind them and handing her the key. As she stepped into the Bronco with his gentlemanly assistance, she noticed how shiny clean it was. "Looks like you spent some of this sunny day washing your car," she stated the obvious.

"And not before it needed it." He closed her door, then went around to get in on his side. "That gravel road leaves it disgustingly dirty, especially since we usually have a heavy dew every night, which makes it even worse."

The drive into Coupeville was a lovely one, with glimpses of the water from time to time, the variety of green trees and shrubs making a viridian patchwork, accented with light and shadow. They exchanged comments about the beauty of the island as they drove. Jan found herself a little nervous. Cade was big, ruggedly attractive, self-confident. His dark brown hair was smoothly brushed from a side part. He had thick dark eyebrows and the most beautiful, long eyelashes. *Why is it that men always get the truly gorgeous eyelashes?* she wondered, and, trying not to stare, turned her head the other way and commented, "Oh, look—a red-winged blackbird."

"I've noticed a lot of them along here; I think it's the cattails that attract them."

"Yes, we see them back by the pond, too. Someone told me you can eat cattail roots."

"Really?"

"Mmm-hmm. And you can get oil from the cattails themselves—the brush part. I don't know if you squish them or boil them in water to extract the oil that way. That's how you do it with mint, you know." Jan noticed the little amused twitch at the corner of Cade's mouth. "I'm sure this is information you've always wanted to hear. That's one of the curses of being a schoolteacher! You never completely turn off." She added, "But just think, if you ever have to live off the land, you'll be able to survive on cattails!"

"Your consideration overwhelms me." He darted a twinkling glance at her.

"Well, I'm glad you appreciate it," she drolly responded.

As he turned into the parking lot of Maud's Mansion, a large, white Victorian home with black shutters and accents, Jan caught her breath. "Oh, I remember driving past here! It's lovely!"

The oversize front door had an oval window with the original beveled glass, a tracing of a clipper ship delicately etched on it. The reception area had burgundy-colored carpeting, with burgundy velvet on the settees. Matching drapes were looped back over white lace curtains, and the wallpaper was flocked burgundy and white. Cade had called ahead for reservations, and they were shown to their table without delay.

The same decor extended into the main dining room, with burgundy napkins contrasting beautifully with the sparkling white tablecloths. Both the floral china and heavy, ornate dinnerware carried out the Victorian theme, and each table had a small nosegay of miniature crimson roses, white baby's breath, and green ferns. Each table as well had on it a candle encased in a dark red glass holder.

"This is lovely, Cade," Jan commented. "It's almost like stepping back one hundred years! How did you happen to run across it? Is the food as good as the decor?"

"This is the first time I've been here," he confessed, "but one of my neighbors recommended it. She assured me the food is *very* good—her nephew is the chef!"

"Ah, it certainly is who you know, isn't it?"

They opened their menus and considered their options. Although the choices were not as extensive as a large restaurant in downtown Seattle would have been, there was a good variety of seafood, beef, pasta, and chicken. They both chose the house salad, with the chef's own dressing, to start. And, since they agreed they'd both had quite a bit of fish recently, grinning at each other, they decided to go with the prime rib. "And," added Jan, looking longingly at the dessert cart being wheeled past them to another table, "I want one of each of those!" She pointed at the array of rich, delectable desserts on the cart.

He licked his lips. "Maybe we should just skip dinner and go straight to dessert?" he asked, raising an eyebrow.

"Hmm. Well, we're grownups—and there are no children here to shock. . . ." She twinkled at him, then heaved a huge sigh. "But no—think what terrible guilt we'd feel afterward!"

"I suppose you're right . . ."

The waitress came then for their order, and they stuck to their original plan, then Cade added, "Oh—and the lady would like one of each of the desserts afterward!"

"Cade!" Jan admonished as she shook her finger at him, then looked up at the waitress. "Not *all* of them. Just be sure the cart is well filled when you bring it by later. We *both*," she said, glancing at Cade, "have been drooling over it!"

As the waitress left, Cade reached across the table to take her hand. "Well," he said with a mock-lecherous leer at Jan, "I will admit I *have* been drooling. . . ."

Jan rapidly fluttered her eyelashes, and said, "Oh, sir! You're making me blush!" And they laughed together, pleased with each other's company.

Not only was dinner delicious, with the bottle of wine Cade ordered, a Washington-produced cabernet sauvignon, complementing the flavors, but the conversation was a light, teasing counterpoint to the meal. The low laughter they shared, the glances warmly exchanged, made it a memorable evening, as both of them forgot the "real world" for the evening.

There was a small dance floor in the adjoining room, reached through a velvet-draped archway, and they shared a dance between salad and the main meal, fitting together perfectly. Jan felt that her feet barely touched the floor, Cade's firm hold making her feel like swansdown. They danced to several dreamy tunes before returning to the table for the entrée.

Later, after choosing dessert, "Death by Chocolate," they returned to the dance floor while the waitress cleared their table and brought their dessert, coffee, and tea. She later delivered a second cup apiece to a small table near the dance floor once they had finished dinner. The offer of a choice of liqueurs or other drinks was declined. The waitress went off, smiling, with the signed credit card slip and a generous tip, while Jan and Cade returned to the dance floor.

The evening passed too quickly, with comfortable silences punctuated with whimsical repartee. Jan couldn't recall an evening she'd enjoyed more. When she went to the ladies room, she sat down on the small vanity stool in front of the mirror and looked at herself in surprise. Who was this woman, flushed and glowing? *I hardly recognize myself,* she thought. *What's happening to me? I'd better be careful I don't get in too deeply. I haven't known him very long.* Then, tossing her just-brushed hair, she thought, *I don't care! Cade is* special. *I want to get to know him better. Well,* she mentally amended, *not* too *much better* tonight! *Just cool it! Not,* she added, *that he's being too fresh, as Mom would say, just . . . be careful. . . .*

Meanwhile, Cade, too, was admonishing himself to caution. Though deeply attracted to and very much enjoying Jan's company, he reminded himself that he was still in the middle of a job, and anything serious would have to wait.

After a few more dances, Jan looked at her watch regretfully. "Cheryl and David will have the children home sometime between midnight and one o'clock." She sighed. "Much as I hate to see the evening end . . ."

Cade murmured his regret, but called for the bill for the refills they'd had, then put her cardigan around her shoulders, leaning down to press his warm lips against the side of her neck. "What a shame . . ."

The drive home seemed shorter, a sizzling quiet between them. They reached Jan's temporary home, and as Cade walked with her to the front porch, his arm around her, she hesitantly asked if he'd like some coffee before he left. "Mmm—I don't think so," he answered. "I think I've had . . . enough . . . to keep me awake most of the night." He looked at her meaningfully. He then led her over to the porch swing. They sat down, dimly aware of the frogs enthusiastic chorus, much more aware of each other. He pulled her closer to him and set the swing moving gently.

Jan curled her legs up beside her and leaned against Cade. He was warm and solid, reassuring and yet exciting, too. "Thanks for a lovely evening, Cade." She sighed. "The food was good, the dancing great—but the company . . . ahh . . ."

His head turned and bent toward her. Jan looked up at him, then everything seemed to disappear when his mouth met hers. As the world started to tilt, she thought dazedly, *Oh, yes, I was going to be . . . uh, oh, yes, cool . . .* And then she stopped thinking to more fully participate in a kiss that surely was tipping the earth completely sideways on its axis.

Time ceased to exist as they clung to each other, lips meeting and parting. Her arms had gone around him, holding him closely to her as he drew her more deeply into his embrace. Somehow the froggy chorus became a doggy chorus, and Jan vaguely recognized Tiger's insistent barking. She drew back slightly, and Cade reluctantly allowed a little space between them, then drew her close and kissed her again. The dog renewed his protest, and the loud, deep bark that Jan had so admired now caused her to sigh. "The dog . . . Cade . . . Mmm . . . Tiger . . ."

Cade lifted his head. "What dog? Are you calling me a dog?" he teased. "Oh—oh, Tiger, you mean."

"Oh, you! He's barking . . ." Another soft kiss. "I think, umm . . . I think he wants out."

"Hmm . . ." Cade sighed. "Yes, I suppose he does. What is it with you?" he teased. "If it isn't kids, it's the dog!" And he kissed her lightly on the nose to show he wasn't angry—only frustrated.

Jan stood up, pushing the narrow strap of her sundress

more firmly onto her shoulder. "My purse . . . uh, my key . . ." They looked around and found it had fallen behind the swing. She fished around in it to find the key, then unlocked the front door. She forgot to brace herself for Tiger's exuberant welcome, and his exit from the house pushed her back against Cade, who also had not braced himself. He stumbled backward as Tiger continued his eager advance, knocking Jan's legs out from under her. Off balance, Cade tried to catch Jan, and then all three of them were on the porch floor, tangled up together. Jan and Cade looked at each other and burst out laughing. He teased, "You really didn't have to fall so hard for me!"

She made a face at him. "In your dreams, Colby!"

They were laughingly picking themselves up, Tiger busy getting his licks in—literally, when the Norris car pulled into the driveway, bringing the twins home. Tiger loped out to the car, barking.

"I hope we aren't interrupting anything," Cheryl teased as she helped get the sleepy twins out of the car. Tiger bounced all around, happy to have all his family home again.

Jan and Cade darted a glance at each other, and Jan hastily said, "Oh, no. Tiger just welcomed us home with too much vigor!" She thanked Cheryl, who gave her an "oh, yeah?" glance, and David for taking the children to the races with them. The twins sleepily repeated their thanks for the great evening.

Cade walked into the house with them. "Need any help?"

Jan smiled at him. "No, thanks, I'll just push them upstairs and be sure they get their shoes off before they crawl in bed." The twins were slowly climbing the stairs.

"I guess I'd better head for home myself," Cade said reluctantly.

Jan looked at him longingly before agreeing. "Yes, it is late. Thanks so much . . ." She walked over to him and put her hand on his cheek. ". . . for a wonderful evening." Her eyes were warm and smiling, her lips slightly parted.

He caressed her face and lips, his eyes still dark with feeling. Then he kissed the palm of her hand and closed her fingers over it, said "Good night, sweetheart," with a crooked smile, and went out the door. Jan stood there for several minutes, her left hand cupping the one he'd kissed, her eyes closed, a dreamy smile on her face. She heard his car drive away, but was still standing there, bemused, when Tiger woofed at the door to come in.

After letting him in, she checked on the twins, then went to bed herself, still floating dreamily on cloud nine.

It rained on Sunday. Jan and the twins slept late, then drove to the store to get the Sunday paper, and the twins talked her into some cinnamon rolls as well. Back home again, the morning passed quietly as they all munched and read, with Trey enthusiastically extolling the fun and excitement of the sprint car races, and Tallie in turn raving about how wonderful Happy, the horse, was, and how she'd just *love* to have one just like him.

Trey talked about one car that had caught their imagination because it reminded them of Tiger—the black-and-orange Number Twelve car. He hinted about going again the following Saturday night, and after the tenth "suggestion," Jan said, "Okay, I got the message, Trey. You want to go to the races again next Saturday night. I'm not saying yes—" He groaned. "—but I'm not saying no, either, at this point." He brightened. "Let's wait until later in the week, okay? It will depend a lot on the weather. I'm not about to sit out there in the rain.''

''But Robby says the races are even more exciting when the track's muddy!''

''Well, I suspect if it rains very much, they probably cancel the races altogether. Surely no one is crazy enough to sit there all night soaking wet! Anyway, enough for now, okay?''

Trey grudgingly agreed, then walked to the window to watch the rain come down. ''There's nothing to do,'' he complained.

Jan stared at him over the top of the newspaper. ''Nothing, hmm? You didn't just go to the races last night after riding the horses most of the day—I'm surprised you can even walk after all that horseback riding! And of course, we didn't have an all-day trip to the aquarium Thursday. Yes, I can understand why you'd be bored—you haven't had anything to do all week. And you don't have *any* toys to play with!'' She hid a smile behind the paper she held as he squirmed.

''He does so have toys,'' Tallie commented literally on the last sentence. ''We've both got lots of stuff!''

''That was just a bit of sarcasm, hon.'' Jan smiled, then added to both of them, ''You've really had a few rather busy days. Why don't you play cards together, or draw and color? Or perhaps you'd like to put together a jigsaw puzzle? And don't forget, we got some books at the library when we got the gardening books. That Hardy Boys mystery you picked up looked pretty good to me, Trey.''

After a little more muttering, Trey got the book out and settled down to read. The rest of the day passed quietly, and Jan surprised them after dinner with a Disney video she'd picked up at the store that morning when they picked up the paper. About halfway through the movie, Jan's parents called wanting to know if they could come to visit the next day. Her father had retired the previous year, and her parents had recently returned from a two-week visit to her older brother, Jim, who lived with his family in Southern California. She and the children took turns talking to them, and the kids were delighted at the idea of Grandma and Grandpa Gregg coming to visit the next day. Jan, too, looked forward to the visit, reminding her parents to bring the pictures they'd taken on their vacation.

The kids were up bright and early the next morning, impatient for their grandparents' arrival. They didn't even need reminding to brush their teeth and hair and make their beds. Not only did Jan have a good relationship with her parents, but so did the twins. The grandparents, of course, doted on the twins and on Jim's eight-year-old son, Jamey, and four-year-old daughter, Cynthia. Jim and his wife, Renae, were both lawyers, sharing a practice in a midsize city in the Bay Area.

They all had a wonderful day together. John Gregg had some teasingly pithy comments about their garden, but smiled while he made them, then helped carry out some of the suggestions he had made. Mary Gregg had brought a bulky care package for the twins, with some new clothes and toys, from both California and Seattle. She had also brought a homemade chocolate cake and the fixings for fried chicken and biscuits for dinner. And, of course, the pictures.

Jan enjoyed being a daughter for a day and letting her folks grandparent the children. Everyone enjoyed the day, and they all walked down to the Sound with Tiger after dinner. Jan was hoping they'd see Cade so she could introduce him to her parents, but they didn't. The children started to talk about him, and Jan's mother asked who Cade was. Her eyebrows raised when Jan and the twins explained they had met him here on the beach but had spent what appeared to be quite a bit of time together.

"He was at our house Saturday night when we came back from the races," Tallie volunteered, "keeping AnJan company."

Mary's eyebrows raised a little higher. "And just what kind of 'company' were you keeping, Janetta?"

Jan flushed a little, "Oh, Mom! Don't sound so stuffy! It's no big deal. I brought Tiger down for his evening walk after the twins had left for the races with the Norris family, and ran into Cade. Neither of us had eaten dinner yet, so we went out for a meal together."

"That must have been *some* meal, Jan," her father teased, "if they were home from the races, but you had just gotten home."

"Well . . . there was a dance floor where we had dinner, so we danced a little, too." Seeking to divert them, she pointed to the west. "Oh, look—there's an aircraft carrier coming in! That's the first time we've seen the carrier from the Everett Navy Base—we've seen some smaller ships, but isn't that *huge!*"

They all oohed and ahhed over the carrier, which was a truly impressive sight. "I wonder if that will be one of the Navy ships that will be tied up in Seattle next month during SeaFair," John Gregg commented. "It would be very interesting to take a tour of it."

Trey jumped on that comment. "Can I come too, Grandpa? I'd *love* to go on that big boat!"

"Ship, Trey, ship," John Gregg, an old Navy man, corrected. "Boats are those little ones out there that you go fishing from."

"Ship," Trey repeated. "Can I come with you Grandpa, when you go onboard?"

"I don't see why not, if the ship's open to visitors."

"How soon, Grandpa?"

"Well, SeaFair doesn't start for another month, but I'll check and see."

"Can I go too, Grandpa?" queried Tallie. "That sounds like fun."

"Sure, pumpkin," John replied. "It will be my pleasure!"

They continued their stroll, then returned to the house for more chocolate cake. About half past eight, John and Mary got up to leave. "The commuter traffic should be through by now." John grinned. "I guess it's safe to head for home." The twins begged them to stay overnight, to no avail. The grandparents had only just returned from two weeks away from their own comfortable bed and weren't ready yet to sleep elsewhere. "How about if we come back next week, instead?"

"All right!" "Wonderful!" "Can you bring another cake, Grandma?"

They all laughed, and Mary assured them she'd bring another cake. "AnJan doesn't know how to make cake, Grandma, only cookies," Tallie confided seriously.

"Now wait just a minute," Jan objected. "I can too make cake—it's just that I thought you preferred cookies! However," she added, "Mom does make better cake than I do." She grinned engagingly at her mother. "By the way, do you have any plans for the Fourth?" she inquired.

Her parents looked at each other, both shaking their heads. "No, I don't think we do, hon," her father answered.

"Well, Phyllis—and possibly her new boyfriend—are coming out for a picnic. Why don't you come too?"

Her parents agreed to the idea. "Traffic shouldn't be too bad," her father commented, "since the Fourth is on a Sunday. The worst of the traffic should be Friday and Monday nights. That means the ferry shouldn't be too crowded."

"You simply can't get him to go *anywhere* in heavy traffic since he retired," Mary teased. "By the way," she added, "will you be inviting your young man for the Fourth?"

"My 'young man,' Mother? What do you mean by that term?" Jan opened her eyes in wide innocence.

"The fisherman, of course—what was his name?"

"She means Cade, AnJan," Tallie pointed out. "You know, Grandma, he's really nice—he talks to us, too."

"Yeah, he's neat," Trey added.

Jan rolled her eyes as the children giggled and her parents looked knowing. "Okay, yes, I'll invite Cade, too. And," she continued, "maybe some of my other friends."

"Well, let me know how many to bake for, dear."

They walked out to her parents' car. "I will, Mom." She leaned over and kissed her mother on the cheek. "Thanks for coming. It's been a great day. And thanks for the goodies!"

"You're welcome, dear." Her mother turned to the twins. "How about some hugs?"

While the children hugged their grandmother, Jan kissed her father on the cheek, and he hugged her close. "Is everything okay, honey? Anything you need?" he asked as he always did. When she was younger, it used to irritate Jan, thinking that her father thought she couldn't take care of herself. But she had come to realize it was part of his love for her, as well as for her brother and sister, that he always asked.

"No, I'm fine, Dad, thanks very much. Drive carefully," she said, tongue in cheek, as that was always his admonition to her. They laughed together, and then he was hugging the twins good-bye, too, and soon Mary and John were driving off down the road while Jan and the twins waved at them.

"I just *love* Grandma and Grandpa!" Tallie enthused.

"Me too!" added her brother.

"Me, too!" agreed Jan, and they turned back to go into the house. Jan saw the dusty blue pickup driving slowly past their property but didn't think any more about it.

Chapter Six

The next morning was cool, gray, and foggy. They could hear the occasional muffled sound of a foghorn emanate from Puget Sound. Tallie and Trey wanted to go again to Robby and Emily's, but Jan objected, pointing out that they'd been there all day Saturday, plus going to the races with them Saturday night. "Don't you think it's your turn to have them here?"

"Well, yeah, I guess so. But we took them with us to the aquarium last week, remember?" Trey pointed out.

"It's so much more fun there than here!" Tallie was close to whining.

"Did you ever think they may think the same thing of here?" Jan inquired. "Most kids prefer going to someone else's house, you know."

"Well, I suppose so," Tallie grudgingly admitted.

"What we *could* do, if you're really so bored," Jan said,

pausing for effect as the children eyed her askance, "is start on those blackberry briars out back."

Trey and Tallie looked at her in shock. "But they scratch!" "Those thorns hurt, AnJan!"

"Or," continued Jan, "we could take all those clods of grass we dug up so we could plant a garden and pile them on the wheelbarrow and take them out back. We could even use them to start a compost pile."

Tallie interrupted hastily, "Can I call Emily and invite her to come play with me?"

"Yeah, and Robby, too," Trey put in.

Jan looked at them wide-eyed, trying not to laugh. "Oh, you'd rather play with them than help me out back?" she said, pretending hurt.

"Aw, AnJan!"

Her smile broke through, and Jan said, "Sure, go ahead and call them."

Emily and Robby were pleased to come play with the twins, and Jan left them happily at it while she went out into the backyard to haul the matted grass clods to the back of the yard near the barn. "Come on, Tiger, I guess it's just you and I," said Jan as she went out the back door, pulling on her gloves as she went. After getting the gardening tools and wheelbarrow out of the garage, she set to work. Tiger roamed to and fro, from time to time taking off to chase something. "Remember, Tiger, no more mice," she said sternly as she watched him race away, nose to the ground.

A couple of hours later, she considered her handiwork. Things were much neater in the garden area, and she was pleasantly aglow with perspiration. In spite of the cool overcast, the activity had left her quite warm. She was pleasantly anticipating a tall glass of iced tea when Tiger came galloping back into the yard, yelping as though in pain. Jan looked up, her first thought that he'd gotten a thorn in his paw or nose, and then she caught a whiff of what his problem really was.

"Oh, no, Tiger—not a skunk!" She raced ahead of him for the back door. "No, no—keep away. No, Tiger—down. *Down!*" she said sternly and very loudly. She managed to edge through the screen door and slammed it and the back door behind her, leaning back against it and panting. "Pee-yew!" She wrinkled her nose. "That's *gross!*"

The children all came clattering down the stairs. "What's up, AnJan?" "What happened?" "Why did you slam the door?" And as they heard Tiger howling and scratching at the door, they said, "Let's let Tiger in."

"No!" she shouted. "Don't open that door! Tiger has had a run-in with a skunk!"

They gazed at her uncomprehendingly, then caught a whiff of the odor that was seeping under the door. "*Pee-yew!*" "Gross!" "Yuck, that's awful!" "Oh, Tiger, how could you!" "What are you going to do, AnJan?"

Standing there feeling frazzled, Jan noted that "what are *you* going to do" carefully. What could she do? What did one do when one's dog encountered a skunk? Something tugged at the back of her mind, but she couldn't quite put a finger on it.

"Where did we put your mother's recipe and household hint books, kids, do you remember? Maybe one of them has a suggestion on how to cope with this contretemps!"

"Contre—what?"

"The smelly dog!" Jan looked around, trying to remember if they'd unpacked the books, but thought not. "Where are the boxes of books, does anyone remember?"

They ran the book boxes down in one of the spare bedrooms, then, through trial and error, found the right household help book. Jan quickly checked the index. "Eureka!" she cried. "Tomato juice!"

The children looked questioningly at her. "We have to bathe him in tomato juice," she said.

"Uh—won't that take an awful lot of tomato juice?" Robby asked dubiously.

"Where would we bathe him?"

Jan considered. "Let's see, kids. First we have to get the tomato juice; I'm pretty sure we don't have any here." She rubbed her forehead. "We certainly can't use the bathtub. I'll tell you what. I'll grab my purse and car keys. Then, while I sneak out the front door, you kids keep Tiger occupied back here. You can open the window and start giving him dog bones, one at a time, if he'll eat them, until I get away." She heard him howling mornfully out back. "And try to do the same thing when I get back, so I'll be able to get back in the house. And behave yourselves while I'm gone, please. I'll be as quick as I can!"

Walking into the living room as she talked, she picked up her purse and keys. "You kids go keep him busy in back while I run to the car, okay?" They nodded and agreed, then ran to the kitchen to follow orders. Looking through the doorway, Jan could see them talking to Tiger and tossing out the bones, one by one, laughing and hollering a lot about the smell.

Jan made it to the car without Tiger catching up to her, but as she drove away, she saw him standing dolefully in the driveway. "Poor Tiger" she said. "It must be awful to be all smelly like that!" But how to clean him up? When she got to the store, she went in to purchase the tomato juice, ending up buying all they had on the shelves—

twenty cans! Surely that would be enough? Oh, yes, and a small metal opener that would make the V-type openings in the top of each can so she could pour out the juice. She also bought some dog soap and vinyl gloves to wear when she did the dirty deed. She told the checker what had happened and why she was purchasing so much tomato juice. The checker and the others who overheard her plight laughed sympathetically. One of them suggested she stop at the feed and seed store to see if they had further suggestions.

She hurried out of the supermarket and drove quickly to the feed store, went in, and told the clerk of her predicament. "No, I can't think of anything that will do it as well as tomato juice," he responded. "Would you like to buy one of our big galvanized tubs to wash him in?"

"I'm not sure he would fit," Jan mused. "He's a Great Dane, you see."

The man whistled. "You really do have your work cut out for you!" Then he continued, "You could maybe put all the juice in the tub and use an old pan or cup or somethin' to pour it on him. Or, we have some long-handled dippers?"

"Well, yes—that sounds like a good idea." Jan purchased the galvanized steel tub and a dipper and quickly left.

Driving home, she tried to plan how they would achieve their object. She couldn't see how it would be possible for *her* not to get equally messy and smelly before the job was through. *Char, you owe me!* she thought. *This is truly above and beyond the call of sisterhood and aunthood!*

When she drove into the driveway, Tiger came running out to meet her, smell and all. Jan looked down at her jeans and sweatshirt, both old and well worn. "Well, I guess this is good-bye to these clothes!'' She found an old scarf in the glove compartment and wrapped her head up, trying to get every last hair tucked in. She also pulled on the vinyl gloves. While she was getting prepared, the kids had managed to call Tiger back around the house, so Jan got out of the car, not bothering with her purse. She went to the back of the van and unlocked it so she could extract the tub and the tomato juice.

She carried the tub over to the middle of the yard with the first four cans of juice. Opening them quickly, she poured them into the tub and went back to the drive where she'd set the other cans, and started carrying them over, too. Uh-oh—here came Tiger, rushing toward her, whimpering and woofing. Jan braced herself and said, ''Down, Tiger!'' very sternly. He dropped to all fours and crawled over to Jan, whimpering, obviously asking for help. ''Oh, you poor baby,'' Jan said, wrinkling her nose at the odor. Gritting her teeth, she grabbed his collar and pulled him over to the galvanized tub. ''Come on, Tiger, it's bath time I'm afraid.'' She tried to hold him still while she poured the tomato juice on him, dipperful by dipperful. Tiger did not appreciate it. The kids had come out to watch and gave encouraging advice and critique from a safe distance.

Jan's hand slipped off Tiger's collar, and she shouted to the kids, ''Look out!'' as Tiger, unappreciative of the tomato juice bath, dashed in their direction. They scattered in all directions, and Tiger stopped for a minute to shake himself. ''Catch him!'' Jan shouted. ''He's not clean yet!'' but the children continued to run in all directions. ''Watch out! Don't let him in the house!'' she called as the girls headed for the front door.

Just then Cade, who had thought to drop in for a little while, heard the shrieks and yelling and came running up the road and into the driveway. "What's wrong?" he yelled.

"Look out!" Jan shouted at him as Tiger raced to greet Cade, who, alarmed, had started running across the grass to Jan. "Don't get near him—"

Too late. Tiger and Cade, each running toward the other, met with a loud smack, and both went down. "Oh, Cade, are you okay?" Jan ran to where they both had tumbled to the grass. Man and dog both sat up, sputtering, Cade with a stunned look on his face. "Wheee-yu! That dog's been near a skunk!" he declared, jumping to his feet.

Jan couldn't help it—she giggled. "Yes, we noticed!" Seeing the look on his face, she quickly added, "I tried to warn you, but you didn't listen!"

Cade was pushing the dog away from him. "Get away, Tiger!" He turned to Jan. "I heard the yelling and thought something was wrong—that you might be hurt."

Jan was still giggling, but managed to stop long enough to say, "Thank you, Cade. And you *can* help." She gestured toward the tub and tomato juice, and smiled at the look of horror on Cade's face.

"Is that blood?" he asked. "Tiger's? Yours?" in a stunned voice.

"No, no—it's tomato juice," she replied. "The book said bathing him in tomato juice would get rid of the smell! I just started," she added, then asked, twinkling, "Would you like to help?" She'd caught hold of Tiger's collar again and started to lead him over to the tub.

Cade looked wryly at his clothes, already liberally splattered in smelly tomato juice, then at Jan, who looked far worse. "Can't get much worse, I guess." He walked over to Jan and Tiger, saluted Jan, and said, "Seaman Colby reporting for duty, ma'am!"

What had been a smelly chore became a laughter-filled smelly chore. The kids came back to cheer and jeer again, but being careful to stay out of the way. The sky had cleared, and the sun shone brightly down on them all. While opening more cans of tomato juice, after emptying the first batch, Jan thought to herself, *I'll never forget this day!*

The children brought the hose around to the front spigot and hooked it up. At Jan's request, Trey got the dog soap out of the van, and Tallie ran to get several big towels. "Be sure they're the oldest, rattiest-looking ones you can find, Tallie!" Jan called after her.

Tiger stood beside them, firmly in Cade's grasp, shivering and whimpering. This was clearly one of the worst days of *his* life. After the last of the tomato juice was dumped out, they ran some clear water in several times to rinse the tub out, as well as hosing off Tiger. Moving to a dry part of the front lawn, they started scrubbing Tiger with the soap. Jan carefully and gently sudsed his face and ears, while Cade did the rest of the dog. Then they hosed him off again, repeating the entire process several times.

"I can't tell if he still smells or not," Cade complained. "I think my olfactory nerves are dead!"

"Hey, kids, come over and smell Tiger. Is it gone?" she asked as they gingerly approached.

"Yeah, he's lots better." "Well, it's almost gone." "He's improved a lot, but you two sure smell!" "Don't let him in the house yet!"

"Tallie, get me the towels, please," Jan urged. She looked at what Tallie had brought. "Are these the worst towels you could come up with?" she asked dubiously. "They look pretty nice. I don't know how they'll wash up after we dry Tiger." She tossed a towel to Cade and took one herself. When the towels were thoroughly soppy, they tossed them aside. Cade unfastened Tiger's collar and turned him loose. Tiger shook himself thoroughly, liberally spraying Jan and Cade some more, as though it were possible for them to get any wetter, then raced around the yard, rolling over several different times in the dry grass. Then he came back and shook himself near the children, who again scattered.

Jan picked up the hose, intending to turn off the nozzle, but it slipped in her wet hand and sprayed Cade, instead.

"Hey! I'm wet enough!"

"Oops! Sorry—it slipped . . ."

He reached over and grabbed the hose from her hand, and turned the water on her. She spluttered and hollered, turning away from him. "No fair! It was an accident!" She turned around, grabbing at the hose, both of them yelling and laughing. The kids were rolling around on the ground, holding their sides as they laughed at the adults. Cade and Jan stopped for a moment, looked at the children, then at each other. "Let's get 'em!" she urged.

"Yeah!" he replied. "Laugh at us, will you?" he roared, running for the kids and spraying them with the cold water. "Take that!" The kids screeched and took off in four different directions, Tiger running among them, barking. As they disappeared around the back of the house, Cade stopped, then turned the nozzle until the water stopped. He looked over at Jan. She looked back at him, and they both started laughing again. He went over and put his arms around her, and they leaned against one another, laughing until they were weak and had calmed down some.

Cade looked down at her tenderly and said softly, "Lady, you really do stink!"

* * *

While showering later, Jan smiled at the the day's events. What had seemed at first a disaster had turned into a fun-filled memory. Before going home to shower (". . . and destroy these clothes!"), Cade had suggested they all go to McDonald's for dinner. The invitation included the Norris children, so they ran home to ask permission, as well as to regale their mother with the skunk episode. The twins, who like Emily and Robby had managed to evade the smell, changed clothes anyway, as they'd become very wet as a result of the horseplay. Tiger was made to stay outside.

Once Jan was cleaned up and smelling better, she found an old blanket and suggested Trey take it out to the garage so they could leave Tiger there while they went to Mc-Donald's. Tiger's ears drooped dejectedly, and although the smell had almost disappeared, no one really wanted to be around him. Jan had bundled her clothes and the vinyl gloves into a large plastic bag, tied it tightly, and thankfully dumped it into the garbage can. Robby and Emily came back, accompanied by their mother.

"I hear you all had an adventure today." Cheryl laughed.

"Yes, *you* might say that," Jan retorted.

"There is still a slight—shall I say fragrance?—lingering hereabouts, I notice."

"Be glad at the timing of your visit!" Jan teased back. "I just hope it never happens again. That wasn't in the baby-sitting class I took as a teenager!"

"Don't feel bad," Cheryl commented. "It wasn't in my motherhood book either!"

Just then Cade drove up in his Bronco. "Anyone hungry?" he called out. "Hi, Cheryl."

"Hi, Cade. I understand you're the hero of the hour—

that you helped corral a wild tiger and doused him—" she was laughing now, "with t-t-tomato juice!"

"You may well laugh, madam! My sense of smell may be damaged forever!"

They dropped Cheryl at her house, then went into town for the children's favorite meal. While standing in line to order, Cade bent his head near Jan's ear and sniffed. "Mmm—you stink very nicely now, honey."

"Yes, I almost bathed in cologne! I'm afraid I'll still be smelling skunk in my sleep." She put her hand on his well-muscled arm. "I can't thank you enough for pitching in to help, Cade. He really was too strong for me to hold onto."

Cade put his hand over Jan's. "I'd like to say, 'My pleasure,' but that might be stretching it a bit." They both laughed. "However, I can safely say *now*, 'My pleasure,' " and he smiled into her eyes.

"Hey, Cade!" "AnJan! They want your order!" "None of that huggy-kissy stuff!" "AnJan's got a boyfriend!"

"I hope so," Cade whispered, then turned to the boy behind the counter. "Did the kids tell you what they want?" The boy nodded, so Jan and Cade gave their orders, too. They took their food to two tables near the windows, looking out at the playground. The kids were told they could go out and play there after they finished their meals. Jan and Cade sat at the next table from the children, taking their time eating. Once the children were playing in the fenced-in area, Cade went back to the counter to get Jan a cup of tea and himself some coffee. They sipped and talked, occasionally glancing out to be sure the kids were okay, then going on to another topic.

Off in the distance, someone was setting off early fireworks. That reminded Jan of the planned picnic for the

Fourth of July, and she mentioned it to Cade. "I hope you'll be able to come join us," she urged.

"I'll be sure I do," he responded. "What can I bring?"

"Well . . . you don't really need to—"

"No, I'd really *like* to, Jan."

"Well, perhaps something to drink? Sodas—perhaps a few beers for the adults?"

"Done!"

Jan looked out at the children, who were still enjoying themselves, then glanced around the room. Through the plants next to them, she saw the man who had tried to sell her a roofing job. What was his name? Johnnie something . . .

Cade noticed where she was looking. "Someone you know?" he asked doubtfully.

"Well, not exactly *know,*" she replied as she watched the man get up and leave. "He stopped by the house the other day and tried to sell me a new roof." She shook her head. "Granted, the roofs aren't in very good condition, but it amazed me that he would just stop by like that. He didn't have a sign on his truck, or a business card or flyer, and when I asked for references, he left."

"Has he been back?"

"Well, no. I think I've seen his truck a time or two, though."

"What kind of truck?"

"Oh, sort of a dusty blue—several years old."

"What make?"

"Oh, I don't know . . . sort of a small pickup—like a Honda or something. Why? Do you know something about him?"

"No, but I don't like the idea of someone like that knowing you're there alone."

"Oh, he doesn't know I'm alone. Besides, I kept my hand on Tiger's collar and let him think Tiger was mean. I figured," she said, smiling, "there was no need for him to know Tiger's really a marshmallow!"

He left the table for a minute, following Johnny Rollins with his trained eyes, saw what vehicle he entered, and memorized the license plate number. "If he comes back anytime, you call me right away, okay?"

"Yes, sir," she responded demurely, a twinkle in her eyes.

He laughed. "Okay, so I'm supercautious—but you can never be too careful!"

The children were having such a good time playing, and Jan and Cade were enjoying their quiet conversation, that they didn't leave for another two hours. Business was not brisk at that hour, so they didn't feel guilty taking up the space for so long. When they headed for home, they first dropped off the Norris children, who chorused their thanks, both for the meal and the ice cream cone they'd enjoyed after they left McDonald's. As they drove into their own driveway, they could hear Tiger carrying on even before they got out of the car.

"What's the matter with him?" Cade asked as they hurried toward the garage. Tiger was barking wildly and scratching at the door. When they let him out, Tiger gave them an abbreviated welcome, then went racing off into the darkness, through the backyard and beyond.

"Oh, Tiger, please don't find another skunk!" Jan moaned. The children started to chase after Tiger, but Cade called them back quickly. "You can't see anything out there. You could trip on something—or meet up with Tiger's friend from this afternoon!"

The twins needed no further reminding, so went into the

house to watch television for a while. Jan and Cade stood near the back door, calling and whistling for the dog. Cade put his arm around Jan's shoulder, and she leaned against him. "Thanks for the lovely evening, Cade," she said softly.

"My pleasure. After all, I felt I owed you something for the fun and games this afternoon." He chuckled.

"And thanks for helping with Tiger, too."

"What are friends for?" he inquired as he turned her in his arms so she faced him.

"Well, good friends are a very rare and precious gift," Jan pontificated in a whisper.

Cupping her face in his hands, he tilted it up toward his. His lips softly touched her eyes. "Very rare," he murmured, then gently caressed her lips with his. "And very precious." Her arms went to his shoulders, feeling the firmness of his muscles. His lips trailed across her cheek to her ear, then back to her pliant lips, stroking his own firm ones back and forth across hers. As he inhaled her fragrance and felt her warmth so near, he bent his head, tipped it just so, put his strong arms around her, pulled her snugly against him, and deepened the kiss.

Jan dazedly realized the earth was again tilting and whirling, and she held to Cade as tightly as she could. Even had she wanted to remain aloof, it was impossible. Something cataclysmic happened when they were this close, kissing and holding each other. Her thoughts stopped, and she only felt, heart beating wildly against the thundering she could feel in his chest.

She would have fallen if Cade had not been holding her so firmly when Tiger returned with his usually enthusiastic greeting, slamming into them, then leaning against them, whining in his throat.

"Tiger," Cade grumbled, "you sure know how to ruin a mood!"

Jan giggled nervously. "He certainly knows how to pick a time, doesn't he?" She patted Tiger on the head, sniffing at him. "Well, he doesn't smell so bad now."

Cade, too, patted Tiger. "He's going to need a new collar, I think. I doubt the old one will 'unsmell.' "

"You're right. I'll be sure to put gloves on while I remove the tags from the old one." She patted Tiger again. "What do you have in your mouth, boy?" she asked, tugging at the bundle he was carrying.

"One of his toys?"

"No, I don't think so." She led Tiger over to the lighted doorway.

Cade took a closer look, then said sternly to the dog, "Drop it!" and reached for the package, which Tiger dropped into Cade's waiting hand. Cade straightened and looked carefully at the package, turning it over and over in his hands.

"What is it?"

"I'm not positive," he said thoughtfully. "Let's look at it inside."

Inside the bright kitchen, Cade examined the package again. "Got a sharp knife?"

Jan supplied it. "What do you think it is?"

Cade made a small opening, then sniffed at the light, powdery substance. "May I have a large plastic bag to put this in?"

Jan got one for him. "What is it, Cade?"

Looking troubled, he answered, "I think it may be—well, I could be wrong . . . ."

"What?"

"It looks like a brick of heroin."

Jan gasped. "But where . . . what . . . how would Tiger have gotten *that?*"

Cade looked levelly at Jan. "I don't know, but I'm going to find out." He glanced at the dog. "I wonder if someone had been around earlier—does he usually bark that frantically and then go racing off right after you get home?"

"Well . . . no. But we haven't had him for very long, either."

"I assume you know nothing about this?" Cade asked gently.

"Of course not!" she replied heatedly. "I've never even *seen* anything like that! The few times I've seen various drugs was when the D.A.R.E. officer came and made a presentation at school, but he just showed small amounts. Surely you don't think I—" She was indignant now. "I would know anything about something like *this?*"

Cade gave her a small smile. "No, of course not. But where," he mused, "would he have gotten this? This is a packaged amount that would be broken down and cut considerably before it would be sold on the streets."

"Are you *sure* that's what it is, Cade? If so, we should call the sheriff."

"Reasonably." He paused, thinking. "Jan—the barn out back. Have you ever seen anyone coming and going from it?"

"No. Why—do you think . . ."

"Well," he said slowly, "when you showed me all the buildings last week, it appeared that perhaps . . . It looked like it had been used recently."

She looked at him blankly. "Used?" She shook her head. "We haven't used it, and I don't think Mrs. Peterson had used any of the outbuildings in recent years. I suppose," she said doubtfully, "she may have had something stored there that had to be moved after she died. . . ."

"Your brother-in-law and sister didn't store some of their stuff there before they moved in, did they?"

"Oh, no; they didn't even sign the closing papers till early May, and then they were busy closing on their place in Bellevue. Besides," she continued, shuddering, "it's so dirty and full of cobwebs and mice and other yucky stuff."

"No, I got the impression you and the kids weren't too keen on it." He thought for a moment. "Let me get a flashlight from my car. I want to take a look out there."

Jan clutched his arm. "No! What if someone is out there!"

Cade grinned at her. "Honey, if anyone *had* been out there still when we got home, Tiger would have routed him out. Hey," he said, leaning his forehead against her, his arms going around her, "it's okay. I'll be all right out there." He gave her a bigger grin, puffing up his chest a bit. "Can't you tell I'm a big macho man? If it makes you feel better, I'll carry a big stick with me."

Punching him lightly on the arm, Jan retorted, "Oh, you! So go ahead and be macho!"

Cade went quickly out to his car for a flashlight. As he circled back past the back door, Jan pointed out he didn't have the "big stick." He leveled a look at her, then, seeing Trey's baseball bat leading against the house, grabbed that, and went quickly toward the barn.

Jan waited nervously in the cheery kitchen after checking on the kids. She decided to heat some water for tea and coffee while waiting, but paced back and forth. It was less than fifteen minutes before Cade returned.

"Did you see anyone? Any traces around?"

"No one. I saw lots of Tiger's paw prints, however, and the side barn door was open."

"I opened it a few days ago for Tiger to chase mice," Jan said, "but I'm sure I closed it again later. What should we do?"

"Tell you what. I'll take this"—he indicated the package Tiger had retrieved—"with me and take it to the sheriff's office in Coupeville. He'll probably want to come out and look around in the morning."

"Surely he won't think *we* have anything to do with it. . . ."

"Honey . . ." Cade started to say something, stopped, then began again. "Tell you what, I'll find out what time he or a deputy will be here in the morning, and I'll come back to be with you. Okay?"

"Okay. What do you think . . . How *would* something like that get . . . Where do you suppose Tiger found it?"

"I don't know, but it's something we'll check out in the morning." He leaned over and kissed her. "Good night, Jan. Be sure you lock the doors tightly—and keep Tiger inside, even if he is still a little smelly."

Jan grabbed at his arm in alarm. "You don't think someone is liable to try to break in or anything, do you?"

"No," he assured her, patting her hand. "Whoever had this originally is probably a long way off." He didn't want her to realize that there had probably been much, much more of the substance originally, if the signs he had seen in the barn were what he thought. "Do you want me to come back and stay the night?"

Jan took a deep breath. "No, I'm . . . sure we'll be fine. Tiger may be superfriendly, but he does *sound* threatening."

"I can come back later if you're afraid to be alone." He grinned at her. "It would be my . . . pleasure!"

"No, it's probably not necessary, and who knows what the kids would think!" she said hurriedly, covering her fear with bravado. "We'll be okay, I'm sure. No, we'll see you in the morning." She didn't mention that she would probably sit up all night, ears alert, baseball bat at the ready.

"You have my number?"

"Yes—and 911 too!"

Chapter Seven

After getting the children to bed, Jan had a quick shower and put on some soft, dark sweats and slippers. She then went back to the kitchen and fixed herself a pot of tea and a sandwich. She had placed a barrier between the kitchen and dining room so Tiger couldn't get into the rest of the house, and he was happy to have her join him in the kitchen. After she petted him for a few minutes, he settled down with a big sigh onto his cedar-filled bed in the corner of the room and went to sleep. Jan stayed awake and worried, but by four in the morning, after dozing off with her head on the table, she saw that the eastern horizon had started to lighten, causing the first of the early birds to start to twitter in the trees, and she surrendered, went upstairs, and crawled in bed for a few hours of sleep. She set the alarm for eight o'clock, not knowing what time Cade and someone from the sheriff's office would arrive.

The twins, of course, were up early, bright and chipper,

a reflection of the beautiful, sunny late-June day outside. Jan groaned as, still in her pajamas and robe, she drank her orange juice. Surely cheerfulness first thing in the morning was totally obscene! Not to mention objectionable. Trey teased Jan about being so sleepy. "Did Cade stay late last night, AnJan? What did you two do? Did you hold hands? Get smoochy?"

"Yeah, Cade was holding your hand at McDonald's yesterday," Tallie volunteered.

"AnJan's got a boyfriend, AnJan's got a boyyy-friend!" Tallie and Trey chanted.

"Oh, shush, you two," Jan responded crossly. "I'm going to go get dressed."

Tallie and Trey looked at each other significantly as Jan left the room. "Wouldn't it be wonderful if AnJan and Cade fell in love and got married?" Tallie sighed. "Then I could be her bridesmaid!"

"You're too young to be a bridesmaid."

"Am not!"

"Are so!"

"Nah, you'd have to be the flower girl and sprinkle flowers all over."

"No, I'm too big to be a flower girl," Tallie objected.

"Then I guess you won't be able to be in the wedding at all," Trey pointed out.

Tallie's lip trembled, "Yes I can! You just wait and see!"

Jan returned while they were still arguing and asked what the argument was about. When told, she sighed. "Kids, Cade and I are just friends, and we're not getting married. And don't you *dare* bring up the subject around him!" she ordered.

They blinked at her tone of voice, then Tallie, her mouth

pulled down, her blue eyes big and tear-filled, said, "But I want to be in your wedding when you get married, AnJan."

"And so you shall, honey, whenever I *do* get married, but that will probably be a long way off. Now, please let's drop the subject, okay? And please don't mention the 'M' word when Cade's around."

"What's the 'M' word, AnJan?" Trey inquired.

"Marriage. Please just put the whole subject out of your minds, all right?"

They heard a car driving into the driveway, and Trey ran to the living room window to see who it was. "Hey, it's a sheriff's car! And Cade's right behind them. What are they doing here?"

"Well . . . Tiger picked something up last night out in the field. It, uh . . . Cade thought it looked as though it might be, um . . . drugs of some kind. He was going to take it to the sheriff, so it's probably about that."

"Drugs?" "What kind of drugs?" "Where did Tiger find it?" "Is Tiger okay? He didn't get sick, did he?" Tiger, of course, had already welcomed them and been petted, but they forgot that in their concern.

"Yes, Tiger's okay. And I'm not sure if it *was* any kind of drug. We'll see what the sheriff has to say, shall we?"

Trey dashed to the front door to open it, his eyes bright and excited. Jan looked from one twin to the other, thinking how differently boys and girls react to things. Tallie was a little hesitant, her eyes vaguely apprehensive, and she stayed close to Jan.

Cade introduce the stocky blond thirtyish man as Deputy Paul Warner. Jan offered coffee or tea, then asked, "What . . . do you know what . . . was in the package? Was it something . . . dangerous?"

Cade and the deputy exchanged glances, then Cade answered, "They're still running some tests, but it looks like it might be heroin, as I suspected. Deputy Warner," he said, nodding at the deputy, "would like to look around outside, if you don't mind?"

"No . . . no . . . certainly, go ahead," Jan said dazedly. "But how . . ."

"We don't know, ma'am," the deputy answered, "but we'd like to find out. I take it this is the dog"—he indicated Tiger—"who carried it in?"

Jan nodded. "Yes, that's Tiger. We don't even know where he was. It was dark out, you know."

"Yes, Mr. Colby explained what happened." They all walked to the back door. "We'll just go take a look around."

"Do you want me along?" Jan asked in a small voice.

"No, ma'am, that won't be necessary. Mr. Colby can show me around, if that's okay?"

"Oh, yes, certainly." She smiled faintly at them. "Thanks, Cade."

Trey, of course, wanted to go along but was not allowed to, much to his disgust. The twins both prattled on about the possibilities, Trey's becoming increasingly wild and gory.

"All right, Trey, that's enough! You're scaring your sister." *And me,* she added silently. She boiled some water and got out some mugs, tea, instant coffee, and milk, just in case Cade and Deputy Warner decided to take her up on the offer she had made for a cup of coffee.

"Maybe they'd like some of Grandma's cake," Tallie suggested.

"It's a little early in the day for that," Jan protested, but added, "but if you think they might want some, please get it down—and some plates and forks."

Tallie bustled around, helping. Jan alternated between watching the clock and looking out the window to see what the men were doing. First they carefully checked the back-yard, then all the outbuildings, staying longest in the barn. After that, they went out behind the barn, to the orchard and pond area, then tramped through the field that abutted Henry Horne's property. They came back across the front yard, then covered the field to the south, bordering the Nor-rises' pasture. Before long they came back toward the house, empty-handed, and stood in the backyard talking.

Jan opened the back door and called out, "Coffee, any-one?" Cade held up his hand in a "just-a-minute" signal, while he and the deputy continued to talk for a few more minutes. Then they walked toward Jan, still talking, looking serious.

Deputy Warner thanked her for the offer of coffee but indicated he needed to get back to the office and make his report. "Mr. Colby can fill you in, ma'am, and if it's okay with you, we may come back again." He started to leave, then turned back. "We'd appreciate it if you didn't say anything to anyone about this." He cleared his throat. "How much do the kids know? We don't want them talk-ing about it either."

"I'll talk to them, Deputy," Cade said. "I think they can be counted on to keep quiet about this, don't you, Jan?" he queried, raising his eyebrows.

"Yes, I believe so, though it may be difficult. They're great Hardy Boys and Nancy Drew fans!"

Deputy Warner left, and Jan and Cade went inside, to be besieged with dozens of rapid-fire questions. Jan thought afterward how well Cade coped with them, not then aware of his background and past practice at fielding inopportune questions. He included them, with very little detail, in the "secret," warning that they must not let whoever had dropped the package know that now the police were in possession of it. In fact, since they didn't have many facts to work with, he asked the kids to stay out of the barn and not to wander too far from the house, and especially not after dark.

As they all shared drinks, with the twins and Cade enjoying some of her mother's cake, Jan could almost see the twins' "I-love-a-mystery" genes come into play as they exchanged frequent glances. She groaned silently, knowing that she'd have to keep a careful watch on them. She mentally debated whether it might be wise to take them to her apartment in Bellevue. After they had gone upstairs to make their beds, she asked Cade that.

He mulled it over, considering safety factors, but having Jan nearby won. "No, I think you'll all be okay. Probably whoever dropped that package won't be back. Actually, the package was rather weather worn—it may have been lying out there, *wherever* Tiger found it, for some time, probably before you all moved in here. They must be aware by now that someone is living here, someone far more active than Mrs. Peterson was."

"Do they have any idea who—"

"We're not sure at this point."

"We? We? What do you mean, *we?*" Jan inquired, frowning, her brown eyes intent.

Uh-oh, Cade thought. "Uh, generic we?" His mind quickly reviewed his options.

She tipped her head to the side, eyeing him warily, thinking back over the past few weeks. What did she really know about him? He was attractive—perhaps *too* attractive for her peace of mind! He appeared to be on vacation, but had he ever *said* so?

He spent a lot of time fishing. Whatever kind of work he did—if he *did* work—he either drew a lot of vacation time or had saved it up. Or—could *he* be one of the bad guys? She shook her head slightly. No, if that were the case, he wouldn't have involved the sheriff's office.

Cade watched Jan's face reflect the trend of her thoughts. He rubbed his bristly jaw and sighed. Confession time—within limits, that would be. "Jan," he began, "I'm going to tell you something in confidence, okay?"

She eyed him dubiously but was impressed by the serious look in his eyes, the stern set to his mouth. Nodding, she agreed. So Cade gave her a brief background sketch of which law enforcement agency employed him and how he had been keeping a watch for the smugglers, not just idly fishing. His lips twitched. "Fortunately I like fishing, both the catching and the eating."

"Yes, well, so do we." She started to ask more questions, but Cade held up one hand to halt the questions, then took her hand in his.

"Jan, I really can't tell you anything more. Will you please trust me?" he asked with a level look.

She gazed back into his eyes, conscious of his warm, firm grip of her hand, almost drowning in his intent regard, and nodded again. "Yes, I trust you, Cade."

He lifted her hand to his mouth, softly kissing each fingertip. "Thank you. I appreciate that. And I trust you to keep who and what I am quiet for now."

Jan smiled tremulously, feeling they'd taken a long step down a road leading . . . where? *Something to think about later,* she thought as Cade released her hand and stood up. "Sorry, honey, but I have to leave—things to do. But either

I or someone else will be keeping a close watch on the house and yard from now on at night, so you don't have to worry.''

Relieved, Jan asked, "Where will you be?"

"Don't worry, we'll be out there, coming and going, even if you don't see us. The idea is *not* to be seen," Cade pointed out.

"Do you have any idea of a timeline on this?" she asked again.

"No."

"Cade, uh . . . would it be easier to keep watch from here in the house?" Jan queried, then added hastily, "There are extra bedrooms, or you could watch from the kitchen, or living room . . . or porch?"

"Not at this time, Jan, but thanks," he said, grinning mischievously, "for the offer."

"But I wasn't offering . . . I only meant . . . Oh, you!"

He gave her a hug, then released her. "I know you weren't, honey, but you're so easy to tease!" He blew her a kiss and went quickly out the front door, yelling "Good-bye, kids" up the stairwell on his way. By the time they clattered down the stairs, he was already outside, getting into his black Bronco.

They turned to Jan with a plethora of questions, most of which Jan couldn't or wouldn't answer. She reminded them of the need to keep quiet about this so as not to interfere with what the law was doing. Jan could see that she had to divert their attention but wasn't sure what to propose. It occurred to her that they had not yet visited nearby Fort Casey State Park. And—Whale-watching! She'd check, and perhaps tomorrow they could go whale-watching on a boat which left from either Everett or Bellingham. When she suggested these diversions, it didn't take long to capture the twins' interest, then enthusiasm. The whales won, hands down.

"Wait a minute," she said laughingly. "I have to get the information about the whale-watching before we can do anything." When she did, it turned out it would take them all day, so she made reservations on the boat for the next day. In the meantime, she told them a little about Fort Casey, which had been built near the turn of the century for coastal defense. One of three forts built, it had also been manned during World War II to guard the entrance to Admiralty Inlet, between Whidbey Island and the Olympic Peninsula, but thankfully no enemy battleships ever made it that far.

Rather than have lunch before leaving for Fort Casey, they decided to take a picnic lunch with them—and Tiger. "We probably should take the camera, too," Jan suggested. "We should get some pictures for your folks." They hastily assembled some sandwiches, fruit, drinks, and the last of the chocolate cake, and set off.

"We could ask Cade to go with us," suggested Trey.

"No, I think he has some project to take care of," Jan replied vaguely.

"Aw, AnJan—we could at least *ask* him!" Tallie persisted.

"No, sweetie—when he left he said he was going to be busy all day. Oh, look at that eagle diving!"

This distracted them sufficiently and led to a discussion of eagles, their habitats, nesting habits, and diet, that continued until they arrived at the park. Although a sunny summer day, it wasn't as crowded as it would be on a weekend. They had fun touring the old fort, climbing in and around the old gun emplacements and looking at the many exhibits. Trey imagined himself firing at passing ships, pretending they were "the enemy."

Because there were quite a few people around, they kept Tiger on his leash, and the twins took turns from time to time running him back and forth. Jan took lots of pictures, finishing the roll. "We'll drop this off to be developed on our way home."

As a distraction, Fort Casey worked very well, and they enjoyed it—and so did I, Jan thought as they headed home. A stop to drop off the pictures led to another stop nearby for pizza. Jan was not very fond of pizza, but the children, of course, loved it. They ran into the Norrises there, who asked them to share their table. The twins were delighted, and Jan was glad of some adult company. In the course of conversation, of course, whale-watching was introduced by Trey and Tallie, who asked AnJan if Robby and Emily could accompany them the next day. "I don't see why not," Jan replied, "if it's all right with their parents—and if there are tickets still available. I'll call again first thing in the morning," she said to Cheryl and David.

Cheryl looked at her dubiously. "Are you sure you're ready for all these kids at once again so soon?" Jan nodded, smiling, and Cheryl continued, "Tell me, do they give you an inoculation before you start teaching so you can't turn off, even during summer vacation?"

The adults laughed. "No, not really. You know yourself," she said conspiratorially, "that if two siblings each has a friend along, things are more peaceful and they entertain themselves," she finished smugly.

"No fair," David said. "Now you know *our* secret!"

They all laughed and continued their light conversation, making arrangements for Jan to pick up Emily and Robby the next morning early enough to get up to Bellingham to catch the whale-watching boat. Jan trailed the Norris car as they all headed home, giving a short "beep-beep" on her horn as they turned into their own driveway.

After she parked the car, she let Tiger and the kids out, glad that it stayed light so late at this time of the year, for of course she hadn't left any outside lights on. She watched carefully as Tiger made his circuit of the yard, in and around the buildings, with a stop here and there along the way. He didn't seem to find anything unusual tonight, and soon was at the back door asking to come in. His dashes in and out of the saltwater today had almost erased the last vestiges of the skunk aroma, so she didn't restrict him to the kitchen tonight. The twins rushed to turn on the TV, and she had Tiger accompany her upstairs to check around. She was glad they'd gotten Tiger, even if he was a problem from time to time.

Jan double-checked the children, then told them she was going to shower. When she was finished, she went on downstairs again in her lilac-flowered shorty pajamas, with a matching light lilac robe. She settled down on the couch with Tallie, who cuddled up close to her. Soon Tallie's head was nodding, and when the sitcom was over, Jan suggested Tallie go on and have her shower, then Trey would have his. It took a while before they were both ready for bed, and then they insisted they were hungry again, so she fixed a dish of ice cream for each of them.

While they were eating, a car pulled into the driveway. Jan was immediately tense, although her good sense told her that if it were the smugglers or anyone else threatening, they wouldn't arrive in such an obvious fashion. However, it was Cade stopping in to check on them and see how their day had gone. He looked at Jan over the heads of the welcoming twins. "Everything okay?" She nodded mutely as the twins, taking the inquiry for them, related how their day had gone.

"Guess what, Cade?" Trey said.

"What?" Cade obediently responded.

"We're going whale-watching tomorrow!"

"Wow! That sounds like fun!" He shot a glance of inquiry at Jan.

"We'll go up to Bellingham," she answered, "and take a tour from there. I haven't done it for years, and Tallie and Trey say they've never been yet. I thought it might be a good"—she paused for the right words—"alternative distraction."

Cade smiled warm approval. "Sounds good to me. Wish I could go too."

The twins, of course, jumped on that, but Cade said he only *wished* he could—he had some work "the office sent out for me to do."

"Besides," Jan interjected, "you'll have Emily and Robby along. Between them and the whales, you won't be bored. And now," she added, "it's time for you scamps to get to bed. Run on up and brush your teeth. Give me a holler when you're ready for your good-night hugs and kisses."

The twins went slowly up the stairs, and Cade whispered in her ear, "I'm ready for a good-night hug!" As Jan turned toward him, he added, "And a kiss," nibbling at her ear. He inhaled deeply, savoring the honeysuckle fragrance wafting from her freshly washed hair. "Mmm, am I ready!"

Jan blushed. "I'm not even dressed . . . and I don't have on any makeup . . ."

"Honey, you don't need any of that. What do you mean,

you're not dressed? You look incredibly well covered to me!''

"You behave, Mr. Colby!" Jan used the most prim, teacherish voice she could summon and shook her finger at him. Just then, the twins called out to her for their goodnight routine, and she went quickly up the stairs.

Cade grinned and wandered into the living room, flipped on the TV set, and sat down on the couch, then searched for the channel with the early news.

Upstairs, Jan listened to see if he was going out the door, but then heard the TV come on. Smiling, she went first into Tallie's, then Trey's, room, giving them big hugs and noisy kisses. This was fine with Tallie, but of course Trey always protested he was ''too big for that sloppy stuff!'' Before going back down, Jan slipped into her room and changed into blue jeans and a soft yellow sweatshirt that read, ''Can Be Bribed With Cookies,'' complete with a picture of a large, chocolate chip cookie. This brought a grin and a chuckle from Cade when he saw it, and he said, ''Me, too!''

"With coffee?" she inquired sweetly.

"I really wasn't hinting . . ."

"I know, but it will only take a minute."

"Well . . . you twisted my arm!"

Jan headed for the kitchen, turning on the overhead light there. She put the water on the heat, then put the cookie jar, shaped like a big teddy bear, in the middle of the table. Cade did not wait for his coffee to start munching cookies. "Did you have any dinner?" she asked him.

Sheepishly, he shook his head. She tsk-tsked and offered to fix him some soup and a sandwich. "You don't have to do that," he protested weakly. "A couple of cookies will hold me till I get home."

"It will just take a few minutes," she assured him as she held up a can of chicken noodle soup, raising her eyebrows at him. When he nodded, she went ahead and opened it and put it in a pan and on the burner to heat. Then she prepared him a turkey sandwich. "Sorry I don't have something exciting like fresh roast beef, but I haven't been doing a great deal of cooking lately. I've been trying to keep the kids busy, which means I stay busy, too."

"You do a great job with them, Jan, and there's no reason you *should* be cooking all the time, too." He smiled warmly at her. "I appreciate your taking pity on me and feeding me *anything!*"

When the food was ready, they sat down at the table. Jan nibbled on a cookie while Cade ate as though he'd not had anything all day. "How are things going, anyway?" she asked.

He shrugged. "Not much new. The package was, indeed, heroin, but of course no fingerprints of interest. Lots of dog saliva, though," he added dryly.

Seeing that he didn't want to talk about it, Jan changed the subject, despite the fact that she dearly wanted to ask about his job and whether his current assignment was typical. So they talked Seattle Mariners, then upcoming elections. Jan refilled their cups, and they moved into the living room. As Jan sat down next to him on the couch, her heart beat faster. He put his arm around her, and she snuggled close to him. They were quiet as they sipped their hot drinks. The room was dim and quiet, too, with the TV turned off.

Cade set his cup down on the coffee table, then held his hand out for her cup, which she gave him. His eyes gleamed as he pulled her closer to him. Stroking her cheek with his fingers, he said, "You have the softest skin I've ever seen—or felt.'' He smiled into her darkening eyes. ''I could drown in your eyes,'' he said, kissing each in turn, ''and your mouth . . .'' His lips moved down to lightly meet hers, touching gently, lifting, then stroking across. Little kisses trailed across to her ear, and he whispered her name, and nibbled at her earlobe.

Jan shivered, her heart thrumming, and one hand slipped around his shoulder, the other raised to his face, cupping it gently, stroking across the cheekbone and down across the raspy cheek, then up to sift through his dark brown hair. She could feel the hammering of his heart against her.

Time both stood still and flew by as they held each other. When Cade's beeper sounded, it took both of them a while to surface. Cade groaned in her ear as the beeper continued its irritating noise. ''I'm sorry, sweetheart.'' He held her close to his long, muscular body for a few minutes more, kissing her more gently, then resting his forehead against her shoulder for a moment. She was still clinging to him, revelling in the closeness and warmth of his body, but the interruption had started her mind working again. She sighed as he pulled away from her and sat up on the edge of the couch, bent over, his elbows on his knees.

She touched his arm gently. ''Are you okay?'' she asked in a small voice.

He grinned wryly at her, and lifted her hand to his lips. ''No, but I'll live. Are *you* okay?'' He paused, then continued, ''I didn't mean to come on so strong.'' He shook his head in wonder. ''I don't usually lose control that way, honey.'' Then he stood up and went to the phone and dialed a number. ''Colby,'' he said tersely, then listened to someone on the other end, and responded in monosyllables before hanging up. Jan, now sitting up on the couch, her arms circling her drawn-up knees, watched him stretch his arms above his strong body and felt her heart turn over. "Trouble?" she inquired.

"Nothing earthshaking, but I'm afraid I'm needed . . . elsewhere." He smiled ruefully at her. "Much as I hate to go . . . Maybe it's better for you, honey." He shook his head again. "You're more potent than brandy, Jan." Walking over to her and pulling her to her feet, he held her hands to his face, turning to place a kiss first on one palm, then on the other. "Ah, Jan, what am I going to do with you?"

She grinned cheekily. "Well, you seemed to know a few minutes ago!" She was tickled at the flush that rose to his cheekbones.

"Hussy!" he teased, putting his arms around her again, holding her close.

She leaned against him, her arms around his waist, as he rested his head against her rumpled auburn hair. They stood like that for several minutes, until he sighed and pushed her away. "Sorry, but I do have to go." They walked to the front door, his arm around her. "Maybe it's just as well, with the kids upstairs. . . ."

"Mmm," she agreed wordlessly.

He leaned over and kissed her forehead, then opened the door. "Take care, sweetheart," he admonished. "Be sure to lock the door." He pulled it to behind him. Jan smiled as she complied. She moved over to the window and waved at him as he backed the car out of the driveway and drove away. Yawning, she double-checked the back door, then turned off the lights and went upstairs. Yes, he was probably right about the timing, but oh, it had been such a delightful interlude. . . .

Chapter Eight

The next morning continued the clear, warm weather, and the twins were excited about going whale-watching. Watching them, Jan wondered if it might be too long a day, as the boat would depart at ten in the morning and not return until five in the afternoon. She phoned to be sure she could get tickets for Emily and Robby, called Cheryl to confirm their plans, then packed the knapsack with snacks, drinks, sunscreen, sunglasses, and sweaters. They were all dressed in the usual jeans and T-shirts, Trey in a teal Mariner one, Tallie in a pink one with butterflies scattered all over, and Jan in a beige T-shirt featuring a frowning orange Persian cat with the inscription, "I *Am* Smiling."

They took Char's blue van and stopped to pick up Emily and Robby, who received a spirited greeting from Tallie and Trey. Jan smiled at Cheryl. "I didn't even think to ask if you'd like to go too," she said apologetically. "Would you? They said they're not yet sold out."

Cheryl shook her head. "Thanks, no. I've got a couple of projects I've been putting off, and this will be a good day to do them." She added puckishly, "Are you sure you don't want to move to the island permanently? You've really been wonderful with the kids!"

Jan grinned back at her. "Ah, but I'm just a temp—in another five weeks I can walk away from it all!" She started to turn the key in the ignition, then turned again to Cheryl. "By the way, do you all have any plans for the Fourth? I have some friends coming out from town, and my folks are going to be here. We're picnicking," she explained. "We'd love to have you join us."

"I don't think we have anything special planned. Let me double-check with David, though, and I'll get back to you. Sounds nice. Let me know what we can bring."

"I hope you can. Well, off we go. See you later—probably sixish. Oh—if we're all starving, we may stop for a bite to eat on the way home, if that's okay with you?"

"No problem. Have fun, all of you. Kids, you listen to Jan and mind her!"

"Yes, Mom." "Yeah, sure." " 'Bye, Mom!" " 'Bye, Mrs. Norris!"

And off they went for a long, busy day in the fresh air. It was an especially gorgeous day to be out on the water, and they were rewarded by seeing two separate pods of orca whales, also known as killer whales, and some seals and porpoises. The orcas, in their vivid, shining black and white, traveled in groups called pods, and researchers kept track of many of them. Tallie and Emily were especially taken with the babies, who stayed close to their mothers.

There were several other children on board too, and after

the first strangeness, most of the kids got along well. There was one four-year-old who was a whiner and a pest, and Jan was thankful that he wasn't her responsibility. The seagulls followed them all day, hoping for handouts—and getting some, too. They could see several of the San Juan Islands as they motored, and whenever they passed another boat, the kids hollered and waved.

After the boat docked and they were once again on dry land, the children pretended to stagger around on their sea legs for a while, then observed unanimously that they were starved. Jan suggested a stop for fish and chips nearby, to finish off their day at sea, so they dined on this messy repast, complete with coleslaw and sodas, finishing off with ice cream cones. By the time they got home after dropping off Emily and Robby, they were all yawning. Tiger was delighted to see them again, and Jan sat on the back steps while he raced around the yard, coming back from time to time to be petted.

Jan followed Tiger with her eyes, then looked around the yard to see if anything seemed different. It didn't. The honeysuckle and roses were still blooming, and as always at this time of evening, the scent was heavy on the slight breeze wafting across the yard. She sighed at the beauty around her. Granted, the house needed some updating, and the other buildings needed repairs, and all needed painting; but what a wonderful place to live and raise a family. Everything was so peaceful that it was hard to believe that some no-goodniks had probably used the barn to store drugs in from time to time.

"AnJan, telephone," Trey called out to her. "It's Cade."

Jan jumped to her feet, a silly smile on her face. *Maybe he'll stop by again this evening,* she thought as she went indoors to the phone. She was to be disappointed, however. Cade was just checking to be sure they were safely home and to tell her he was going to be tied up all evening. He gave her a number where he could be reached, however, and asked if she had the number of the sheriff's office. "I can look it up," she assured him, but he quoted her the number and made sure she wrote it down.

"How was the whale-watching?" he then asked.

"Oh, wonderful. We saw some orcas, some seals and porpoises—and lots of seagulls! It was a beautiful day out on the water. But then you were probably at your usual—um, location—and know how nice it was!" she teased.

"Yes, but the company wasn't nearly as distracting," he countered.

"Catch anything?"

"Yeah, some bottomfish and a dogfish. Turned 'em all loose, though."

They chatted for a few minutes more before he sighed and said he'd have to hang up. "Back to work." He sighed again, then added, "Jan, do you suppose we could spend some time together Saturday night? Maybe dinner, or dancing? Or—hey, the Mariners are in town. How about driving into Seattle and catching a game?"

"Oh, Cade, that sounds wonderful! I don't know—let me do some checking. I haven't been to a game yet this year!" *Not to mention I want to spend more time with you—just you and me!* "I suppose," she mused, "if worst came to worst, we could drop the kids at my folks' in Lynnwood. It wouldn't be much out of the way."

"Sure, that would work out fine," Cade agreed.

"Or perhaps the Norrises would 'adopt' them again for the evening. I'll see what I can do."

"Good! Gotta go, honey; someone needs me," he said. "See you soon. . . ."

"Good-bye." But she was talking to the dial tone. *I need you, too,* she thought. *Wait a minute, Janetta, let's review that phrase again. What's with this need? Want, maybe; like—well, a lot. But let's not go overboard on this. This guy is pretty involved in his work, and it does seem to come first with him. Don't get your hopes up. Don't get hurt!*

"Is Cade coming over?" Tallie asked.

"No, dear, he was just checking to see if we got home all right."

"Yeah, sure!" Trey teased. "What time did he go home last night?"

"Oh, not long after you kids went to bed." She hadn't checked the clock after Cade left and truly didn't know how long he'd been there. *Too long and not long enough!* she thought. "He missed dinner, so I fixed him a soup and a sandwich. And, of course, my famous, my *fabulous,* chocolate chip cookies!"

Reminded of the cookies, the twins decided they sounded good and raided the cookie jar. "Teddy's almost empty, AnJan," Tallie complained.

"Oh, yes . . . We'll make some more tomorrow, okay?" she answered absently. "Perhaps," she said with a silly grin, "a double batch!"

Squabbling over who should have the last cookie, the twins missed the grin but agreed with the conclusion. "Maybe even a *double* double batch, AnJan!"

After the twins were tucked in for the night, Jan went back downstairs and looked around at the evidence that the house had not received even a lick and a promise during the week. "It has that lived-in look, doesn't it, Tiger?" Well, tomorrow morning, at least, would be devoted to cleaning, laundry, and baking, she decided. "And the kids can help," she murmured. She let Tiger out for another tour of the yard, then he followed her upstairs. He went into Tallie's room for the first half of the night, and Jan went on to shower and get ready for bed. *I have to admit, I feel much safer with Tiger here—and especially having him upstairs. Char's probably not going to be happy about the dog spending the night in the twins' bedrooms, though. Oh, well.* She shrugged. *Not my worry. I do hope, though, that they catch the drug smugglers before Char and Tom get back.*

Friday brought a gray, drizzly rain, which made it easier to stay indoors and tend to some housekeeping. The twins did their usual grumbling, if for nothing more than appearance's sake. By lunchtime, Jan was well pleased. Vacuumed, dusted, and "picked up," the living room gleamed, its earth tones revitalized, the orange, pumpkin, and persimmon pillows plumped up, furniture polished. Even the windows had been Windexed and shone behind the sheer ecru curtains. The beds had all been changed, with the sheets still in the dryer. They had been preceded in both washer and dryer by three other loads of laundry. And Jan laughed at the twins, saying that they had "enough cookies for a siege," then had to explain a siege.

Over toasted cheese sandwiches, orange sections, and milk, they discussed the Fourth of July picnic. Cheryl had phoned to say that they would be pleased to join them and had offered to make a big bowl of potato salad. They prepared a typical menu for the Fourth—hamburgers and hot dogs, with lots of catsup, mustard, pickles, onions, tomatoes, lettuce, and olives; potato salad, and baked beans. Grandma would bring a big chocolate cake, and Grandpa was a past master at the barbecue. Cade was bringing drinks. "I'll call Phyllis and see if they'll bring some chips and dips," Jan mused. "I'll fix some carrot and celery sticks, too—we need *something* healthy!" She laughed as the twins made faces and threatened to throw things at her. "And we'll put out a bowl of fruit."

"And marshmallows, AnJan, to roast over the barbecue! Can we have marshmallows, too?"

"Sure," she answered good-naturedly, "why not?" She added a number of other items to the grocery list she was compiling. "Why don't we go to the supermarket after lunch and load up before it gets any later? There's usually quite a rush before a holiday weekend."

By the time they returned from the store, they not only had purchased everything on the list, but many things *not* on it, including three flavors of ice cream. They had also made a stop at the library, returning the books they'd finished and picking up a few more. Later that day, Jan called her parents to see if they would keep the children Saturday evening. Delighted with the idea, Mary suggested the twins stay overnight, and Mary and John would bring them out with them Sunday morning when they came for the picnic. "That is, of course, if you promise to behave yourself, young lady," her father chimed in on the extension phone.

"Dad!" she exclaimed, embarrassed. "You know I *always* behave myself!"

"Well, I certainly hope so, dear," her mother said. "John, stop teasing!" Jan could hear her father mutter "I wasn't teasing" as her mother asked what time she could expect them Saturday.

"Hmm . . . the game begins at seven-thirty, and traffic . . . and parking. . . . How about if we drop them off about five-thirty? I'll double-check with Cade. Would that be okay with you?"

Assured that it would be fine, Jan and her mother chatted a few more minutes before hanging up, and Jan turned her thoughts to preparing dinner. She oven-roasted chicken pieces for dinner and baked some potatoes. Together with a big tossed salad and ice cream and cookies for dessert, it was a nice meal, and they were all ready for a quiet evening at home once the dishes were washed.

While the twins were arguing mildly over the dishes, Cade called. "Anything new?" Jan inquired.

"We're following up on a couple of leads," Cade answered, "but we won't know for a while how good they are. What did you do today?" he asked.

Jan reviewed the mundane day she and the twins had spent. "Oh—and we made some more chocolate chip cookies," she teased.

"Mmm—I wish I could come sample some," he declared regretfully. "But I'm going to be tied up most of the evening." More cheerily, then, "But it looks like I'll be able to get away tomorrow evening. I called for tickets this afternoon. Since it's the Bluejays, lots of Canadians will be coming down from B.C., but I was able to get some fairly decent seats. Any luck in the baby-sitting department?"

"My folks said they'd be glad to have them and offered to keep them overnight, then bring them back Sunday morning for our Fourth of July picnic."

"All *right!*" Cade exclaimed, pleasure evident in his voice. "I can hardly wait."

"However, Daddy warned me that I should behave myself," Jan added.

"Well, of course—what else?" Cade asked innocently, then chuckled wickedly.

"Oh, you!" she exclaimed.

She heard Cade speak to someone at his end, then he said to her, "Sorry, hon, I've got to run. What time shall I pick you up?"

"I told my folks we'd probably get there about five-thirty, if that's all right with you. That should give us time to get to the Kingdome before the game starts. Let's see," she figured, "if we catch the four-forty-five ferry—well, how about four o'clock? Does that sound about right?"

"Sounds good. See you then." Then he murmured, almost under his breath, so she wasn't positive she heard it, "If I can wait that long."

" 'Bye," she said again, to the dial tone.

"Who was that?" Tallie asked as she drifted into the living room.

"Cade, checking on what time we need to leave tomorrow. By the way, don't forget to pack your pj's and toothbrushes tomorrow sometime—and a change of clothes for Sunday."

"What time will we get home Sunday?" Trey asked.

"Well, if I know your grandfather," she muttered under her breath, "he'll probably be up with the birds to get out here thinking to catch me in flagrante delicto!"

"Delict—what?"

"Oh, wanting to get here in time to have some of our delicious cookies!" Jan said hastily.

Just then, the phone rang again. *Saved by the bell,* she thought as she lifted the receiver. It was Char and Tom calling from New Zealand. The twins were thrilled to pieces to talk to their parents again, and the conversation lasted close to an hour. The twins had lots to tell their parents. *Well, we have been doing a lot, at that,* Jan thought, then heard Tallie say, "AnJan has a boyfriend!"

Jan rolled her eyes and then shook her head at Tallie, frowning ferociously.

Tallie giggled, then went on to tell her parents about Cade, so when Jan finally had her turn on the phone, her sister's first question was, "Who's Cade? Where does he live? What does he do? When did you meet him? What does he look like?"

"Whoa, there, Char! Hey, he's sort of a neighbor, at least for the summer. He's a very nice man."

"A very nice man!" her sister retorted. "Now tell me the rest of it!"

Jan gave an edited and conservative version of the "acquaintance" with Cade. And she was careful not to say anything about the package Tiger had discovered, and its import. No point in alarming Char and Tom when they were so far away. Besides, with Cade nearby, she really wasn't very nervous. She returned the phone to the twins, one at a time, and when Trey started off, "Guess what Tiger found?" she shook her head and held her finger to her lips, indicating silence on the subject. Trey instead paused, then told his parents about the skunk incident. When Tallie had her turn on the phone again, she told her parents about the Fourth of July picnic scheduled for Sunday. "But tomorrow night we're going to stay at Grandma and Grandpa's,'cause AnJan's going out with Cade."

So then, of course, Jan had to get on the phone again to explain the plans, and add, "And yes, I'll be a good girl, just as Dad told me!"

In New Zealand, Char giggled. "Well, not *too* good, I hope!"

Again, after they hung up, the children were rather quiet. They'd never been parted so long from their parents, and although they had been taking it in stride, talking with their mother and father had made them quietly sentimental. Jan sat between them on the couch, talking with them, her arms around them. She started to tell them about some of the mischief she, Char, and Jim had gotten into when they were young, and soon they were all laughing. When Jan asked, "Who'd like some popcorn?" both exclaimed, "I do!" and they all went to the kitchen to prepare some in the microwave. Jan had checked the TV schedule while the twins were talking to their parents and located a funny movie aimed primarily at children, and soon they were back on the couch watching the movie and munching popcorn.

Saturday was a busy day. The twins were again invited down to the Norrises' to play and to ride horses, and Jan was busy preparing for the picnic the next day. In addition to food, she'd gotten plenty of paper products so they wouldn't have a lot of dishes to wash afterward. Before the twins left, she had them help move the picnic table to a more appropriate spot in the backyard and get out the remaining lawn furniture from where it had been hastily stacked in the garage. Fortunately there were several plastic occasional tables that would also come in handy. Then they had to move things around a lot to extract the barbecue and its fuel.

Jan scrubbed down the tables—and chairs, too, where necessary. She searched for the red-checked terry tablecloth that Char usually used for picnics and finally found it in one of the yet-to-be-unpacked boxes upstairs. While looking for it, Jan thought to herself that she should probably unpack the linens and put them in the upstairs hall linen closet for Char. Phyllis called about noon for directions, since she'd lost the ones already given her, and asked if there was anything she could bring besides chips and dips.

Jan told her what the menu was, and Phyllis said, "Watermelon—a picnic's not a picnic without Watermelon!"

"Okay, fine—sounds good. Better buy one already chilled if you can, because I don't know if I'll have room in the fridge to store it. I'm so looking forward to seeing you, Phyll! It seems like a year!"

"I know—I've really missed you, too."

They chatted for about half an hour, Phyllis with a lot to say about Roy, and Jan responding with some details about Cade. "I'm really attracted to him, Phyll. He has that—oh, I don't know—that certain something. There are sparks when we're together. I've never felt this way before!"

"Sounds serious, my friend, but don't do anything rash until I can check him over tomorrow."

"I'll try." Jan sighed. "We're going to see the Mariner game tonight."

"Taking the twins, too?"

"No, we're dropping them off at Mom and Dad's— they'll bring them home again tomorrow when they come for the picnic."

Phyll was quiet for a moment. "Why, you rascal!" she chided. "You mean you and this hunk are going to be there all alone tonight when you get home?"

"No . . . well, yes, I guess so. But he's not staying here! You know me better than that!"

"I do, but does he?"

Jan considered that question later as she dressed for the game. The twins were busy getting ready too, and packing their jammies and other things they considered essential to spending the night with their grandparents. She paused while brushing her hair and looked herself in the eyes. *Does*

Cade know me well enough to know I wouldn't . . . She paused and considered. Hmm . . .

I guess I'll just have to play it by ear. I can always say I have a headache! She grinned at her reflection, then continued brushing her wavy auburn hair. She noticed how much it had grown the past couple of months, so that it was now almost down to her shoulders. Cut it again soon or let it grow? she pondered as she applied her lip gloss.

She twisted and turned to see how she looked. She wore dark blue jeans, an embroidered denim vest open over a long-sleeved, light-blue checked shirt, tucked into her snugly fitting jeans. Small silver hoops in her ears and three silver chains of varying lengths around her neck. A Mariners' baseball cap for her head, and a quick check of her purse, and she was ready. She started for the stairs. Then she returned for a light denim jacket, just in case. Her heart started beating faster as four o'clock approached. When she passed the twins' rooms, she reminded them time was getting short, then went downstairs to check that Tiger had plenty of food and water.

Cade was a few minutes early, and there was a bit of a bustle getting the twins out the door. With the twins in the backseat, Jan and Cade couldn't have much of a conversation, but as he answered the children's rapid-fire questions about what the law was doing about the heroin, she was able to look her fill of him, more interested in the view than the subject, although she did notice he was able to answer ambiguously and then lead the conversation in a different direction. Dressed, like her, in jeans, he also wore a navy polo shirt and had tossed his jeans jacket on the seat between them.

Once on the ferry, the twins scrambled up the stairs first, heading for the forward deck. Cade followed Jan up the narrow stairs, admiring the view. "You look good enough to eat," he murmured as they emerged in the main lounge area and he put his arm around her. "And you smell good enough to eat, too," he said as he nuzzled her neck.

"Cannibal!" she teased, slanting a look from her laughing brown eyes to his slumberous blue ones. He snapped his teeth in a mock snarl, then nipped lightly at her ear. "Mmm, yum," he whispered.

As they went out on the deck, she admonished him, "Behave now!" with a ferocious scowl.

The thirty-minute ferry ride went quickly, and soon they were back in the car, heading for the Gregg home in Lynnwood. Jan introduced Cade to her parents, and they had a few minutes of general conversation, interspersed with excited comments and appeals for their grandparents' attention from the twins. Jan and her mother then exchanged a few remarks about the next day's picnic, so Jan didn't notice her father give Cade a level look and say, "You go carefully with my daughter, young man."

"Yes, sir," Cade responded, struggling to hold back a grin. "You can trust her in my care, sir."

John Gregg shot him a skeptical look, but Jan came over to kiss her father on the cheek then, saying, " 'Bye, Dad and Mom. We'll see you tomorrow! 'Bye-bye, Tallie and Trey—you behave for Grandma and Grandpa."

"*You* kids behave," her father muttered, and her mother said "Hush, John! You'll embarrass Jan."

Fortunately Jan missed her father's pointed comment, but Cade smothered another grin as he said, "Nice to have met you both. We'll see you tomorrow."

In the car and on their way again, Cade reached for Jan's hand. "Your father's rather . . . protective, isn't he?"

"Yes, he finds it hard to realize we're all grown up. He

almost always asks any of us, when he calls, if we need anything. I guess parents always remain parents, and to them we're always children.''

"It's nice to have caring parents. I've been lucky that way, too, although my folks don't live nearby—Dad's retired from the Navy, and they live down near San Diego."

"Yes, but there were times in high school when being an orphan sounded pretty good! He always vetted my dates—scared some of them so badly they never asked me out again!"

"Yes, I can just . . . picture that," Cade responded, smiling wolfishly at her.

She fluttered her eyes at him, pursed her lips, and asked, "Did he scare *you* off?"

"No way!"

"Good!"

The baseball game was exciting, well played with good pitching, and the Mariners won it in the bottom of the ninth. Jan and Cade, like everyone else departing the Kingdome, were cheerful and still smiling as they reached the car.

"It's going to take a while to get out of this parking lot," Cade cautioned as he turned to some soft background music on the car radio.

"That's okay; I'm in no hurry." She got her hairbrush out of her purse and quickly brushed her hair, then dabbed on a touch of gloss to her lips. "There!"

Cade had watched her in fascination, then caught her hand and said teasingly, "You do know that I'm going to have to kiss that off, don't you?"

Jan opened her eyes very wide, then fluttered her lashes at him. "No—why do you have to kiss me?"

"Just because . . ." He dipped his head and touched his

lips to hers lightly. ". . . because they're *there!*" He kissed her lightly again, then drew back.

"Is that like having to climb Everest—because it's there?"

"Oh, no, this is much more . . ." He kissed her lightly again. ". . . compelling. Mmm—you taste good. . . ."

A group of teenagers passing their car banged on the hood several times, hooting and whistling, startling Jan and Cade.

"Oh, dear, I hope those weren't any of my students!" She groaned.

"Why, aren't teachers allowed to have a life of their own?"

"Yes, but preferably not in public," she answered wryly.

Cade started the car and started to edge it forward. He gave her a slumberous glance. "We'll finish this later," he warned.

Once they were on I-5 headed north, Cade asked Jan if she'd like to stop for something to eat before catching the ferry back to Whidbey Island. Jan asked, "Won't we miss the last ferry if we do that?"

"We can always drive around," he replied. He ducked his head to look up at the sky. "Just look at that moon—and the stars! Besides," he added, "they'll be calling me for *something* once I'm back on the island, you can be sure of that!"

"Do you have to check in when you return? Don't you get regular days off?"

"Normally I do, but this is sort of an all-hands, with no designated hours, project."

Reminded, Jan asked, "How are things going, really? Have any of the leads you mentioned panned out?"

He was quiet for a moment, phrasing his answer. "Have you ever heard of 'China white'?" he asked her.

"No, I haven't," she answered. "Is that some kind of porcelain?" she queried, wondering at his question.

"It's a new kind of heroin that's being seen in our area, although so far more of it has turned up in B. C. than here. There have been almost a dozen deaths recently from China white in British Columbia, mainly in Vancouver."

"Oh, I do remember something about several people dying up there from heroin overdoses, now that you mention it."

"This China white heroin is so pure—either uncut or cut very little—that some of the people dying from it still have the needles sticking in their arms or legs, wherever they've injected, when they die. It's that quick."

Jan shuddered at the thought. "But don't they *know* how dangerous it is?"

"No, they're probably used to the Mexican brown that's usually available on the streets, which is bad enough. The authorities have been warning the addicts up in Vancouver about how lethal this stuff is, but when someone is after a quick fix, they don't want to hear that. I don't know if you're aware of it, but the police up there don't arrest as many users as we do; they even have a needle exchange available for them."

"I didn't realize that. I know they do something like that in Tacoma . . ."

"But on a much smaller scale. Anyway, it's very important that we cut this stuff off if we can, or at least limit it as much as possible. But having so much shoreline makes it tough to watch everywhere. Actually, as you're aware, it's been impossible to keep it out. We get some info from informants. There are some people we know are involved, but we don't have enough proof. It's incredibly frustrating—we need so many more agents and officers and much more money to keep it out; but as long as people are willing to spend the money to use it, someone will do whatever it takes to get it to them.''

"It must be terribly frustrating."

He nodded grimly. "It is. I had a kid brother who got into drugs in his late teens, when he was in college."

"Oh, no!"

"Fortunately we got him into a drug rehab program pretty fast, and he's been clean for the last seven years; but something like that really brings it home to you."

Jan placed her hand on his arm in a comforting gesture. "I know how awful I'd feel if my brother or sister—or the twins—got involved in drugs."

Cade lifted her hand and kissed it before putting it back on his arm. "Thanks, honey." Then a surprised look crossed his face. "Well, so much for stopping for something to eat! I must have been on automatic pilot. Here we are at the ferry." They both laughed as he drove the Bronco onboard. "Well, at least we can go topside, and I'll treat you to some coffee. Unless you'd like to stop somewhere after we get off the ferry?"

"No, this will be fine," she replied as they reached the top of the stairs. "I ate plenty at the game! Those hot dogs always smell so good, but they too often just seem to sit there afterward, barking."

They decided instead to have hot chocolate—with marshmallows—and took their drinks to the aft deck with them. Leaning against the railing, sipping their hot chocolate, arms about each other, they enjoyed the drink and the closeness. As the ferry moved out into Possession Sound, the stars and moon seemed very close. Jan murmured, "Does this seem like déjà vu all over again to you?"

Cade chuckled. "Yes, Yogi, it does," he said in response to her quote of a phrase made famous by the great Yankee catcher, Yogi Berra, several decades earlier. When they finished their drinks, Cade took the empty cups and tossed them in the trash. When he returned to where she still leaned on the railing, he stood behind her and put his arms around her waist. She leaned back against him, her arms resting on his. They were quiet for the rest of the trip, enjoying their closeness and the beauty of the night.

They held hands on the drive home, both aware of the sparks between them. As they turned in to her driveway, Jan rushed into nervous speech. "This has been a wonderful evening, Cade. Thank you so much . . ."

He turned toward her and kissed her hand before getting out of the car. He smiled tenderly and said softly, "It's okay, Jan—I'm not going to rush into anything we're both not ready for."

She smiled gratefully. "Sometimes it's like you can read my mind."

As he opened his door of the car, they both heard Tiger fiercely barking and howling in the house. They glanced at each other, then they both jumped out of the car and ran toward the house. Cade paused to grab his flashlight. "Hurry, Jan—let's get the door open." She fumbled in her purse for the key. He grabbed it out of her hand and quickly opened the front door. Tiger came roaring out of the house, circled them once, then raced around the house toward the barn. Cade took off after him, saying, "Go inside and lock the door, Jan!"

"Cade—be careful!" she called after him. She stood there hesitantly, then went in and closed the door, turning on lights as she progressed through the house. At the back door, she turned on the outside lights. She could see Cade's flashlight bobbing about, then going into the barn.

I wonder if I should call 911, she mused. *No, Cade would have said if he wanted me to call anyone.* She opened the back door a crack. Tiger was no longer barking. Was that good or bad? She closed the door again, and rubbed her hands together, shifting from one foot to the other.

Then she saw Tiger heading for the house. She opened the door again. Whatever had caused him to take off the way he did was evidently gone. "Cade?" she called. "Are you okay? Tiger's here by the back door."

"Yo!" he called back. "I'll be right there." And soon the flashlight was bobbing and sweeping across the yard as he, too, headed for the house. When he came into the kitchen, he turned off the flashlight.

"Did you see anything?" Jan asked anxiously.

He looked at her strained face and quickly put his arms around her. "No. And all I heard was Tiger barking and carrying on. He seemed to be chasing something back through the orchard. Any cats in the neighborhood?"

"I haven't seen any. How about the barn? Did anything look . . . out of place?"

"No, it didn't look any different than last time I was in there." He didn't mention having sprinkled an odorless powder inside the barn when he'd been there earlier in the week. The barn was so dusty and dirty no one would notice, but anyone walking through it would have traces of it on their shoes. This would show up under a special light. Perhaps not a defensive ploy, but possibly helpful at some point. "I'll come back in the morning and look around some more. I'll even," he said, looking at her roughishly,

"be happy to . . . spend the night. My specialty is comforting maidens in distress," he teased.

She smiled faintly at his teasing while her mind considered his offer, wondering which was more dangerous to her
well-being—a possible prowler or this man who upset her
equilibrium and made her heart pound like a jungle drum.

Tiger interrupted, bumping against them in a request for
attention, reminding Jan that he hadn't been greeted prop-
erly when she arrived home. She pulled away from Cade
abruptly and leaned over Tiger. "Sorry, boy, but you did
go rushing out before I had a chance to say hello!" Tiger
leaned against her, his tail beating a tattoo on the floor as
he sat down on her foot, his doggy eyes adoring her. "Well,
whatever it was, Tiger, you certainly chased it away." She
stroked the dog's head as Cade wryly observed to himself,
Upstaged by the dog again!

Cade watched Jan, aware that she was nervous. He asked
softly, "Would you like me to stay, Jan? I promise"—he
held up his right hand—"to behave myself—scout's
honor!"

She raised relieved eyes to him. "Thanks, Cade, but I
think I'll be okay. Only—would you check upstairs before
you go?"

Cade walked up the stairs with her and checked all the
rooms, closets, and under the beds. Then they said good-
night reluctantly.

Jan's thoughts and dreams that night were of Cade. It
was Tiger who spent that night with her—on the floor beside the bed.

Chapter Nine

Jan didn't sleep very well that night, waking, ears alert, more often than she liked, but all she heard were Tiger's snoring and snuffling. She got up early, if bleary eyed, and drank three cups of strong tea before she felt able to function normally. She looked at the lists she and the twins had prepared, and picked up where she had left off on Saturday. The day promised to be clear and beautiful again, with a light breeze blowing in from the Strait.

She was carrying out tableware, paper plates, and napkins when Tiger began to bark. As he rushed toward the honeysuckle-covered fence edging the north pasture, she looked to see what was causing him to carry on so. An elderly, unshaven man, in old bib overalls and a brown plaid flannel shirt, was crossing the field. A farmer-type straw hat was jammed on his head, his faded blue eyes sparking with anger. "Git away from me, you blankety-blank dog!'' he said crossly as he waved a stick at Tiger. ''Go on, git!''

''Hey, that's *my* dog you're trying to hit! Leave him alone!''

Before she could ask who he was and what he was doing on her property, he verbally attacked Jan. ''I warned them kids to stay off my property, missy, but they didn't listen!''

''Whoa, wait a minute. Who are you?''

''Name's Henry Horne, and I live yonder.'' He nodded his head to the north. ''I warned them kids not to come over—''

''And they haven't!'' she interrupted.

''Yes they did! Last night—heard 'em runnin' through my trees!''

''Well, for your information, they weren't even *here* last night, Mr. Horne!'' Jan retorted. *And put* that *in your pipe and smoke it,* she added mentally.

''Sure they was. Heard 'em myself. They they took off in an old pickup!''

''Mr. Horne, my niece and nephew are only ten years old and don't even know how to drive. And besides, as I told you, they were *not* here last night. They were with my parents in Lynnwood. If there *were* some kids down there, they weren't from here!'' Curious, she added, ''How do you know they were kids?''

''Musta been. Hear 'em every now and then. Haven't been able to catch 'em yet, but I will. You can bet I got my shotgun loaded, too!'' he added, frowning, his pale eyes peering out from under the bushy white brows.

''Well, they weren't from here!'' Jan again stated. ''And I'd be careful about making threats like that.'' A thought struck her. ''You say you heard a truck, too?''

"Yup! Maybe 'twas *you* out there—you and maybe some fancy-pants city guy with you."

Jan clenched her jaw, glaring at him. "No," she replied icily, "it wasn't me, either. Have you called the sheriff's office?"

Horne snorted. "That lot! All they're good fer is riding around with lights flashin'!" He turned toward home. "You keep them kids and that there dog"—he pointed the stick at Tiger, who was by now sitting beside Jan, her hand on his collar—"off my place, missy!"

"They haven't *been* on your place!" she retorted loudly, but all he did was give a loud snort of disbelief.

Jan clenched and unclenched her fists, even stomped her foot, she was so upset with the man. "Can you believe the nerve of that man?" she asked the dog as she and Tiger turned back toward the house. Then a thought occurred to her, and she addressed her question to the dog again. "Tiger, did you take off into that field last night when I let you out? But no," she mused, "if that had been the case, Cade would have searched in that direction."

She was still disturbed as she went back into the house. The longer she thought about it, the more she wanted to call Cade. Was it just some kids aggravating the old man—or had they been connected with the drug smugglers? "I'll tell Cade about it when he gets here later." She loaded the tray with tablecloth, salt and pepper shakers, and other non-perishable items and carried that out to the picnic table, too. She opened several cans of baked beans, put them in Char's large Crockpot, added various seasonings, and plugged the pot in, all the while continuing to mull over what Henry Horne had said.

I'm going to call Cade now, she thought. *Maybe it's connected and maybe it's not, but someone in authority should check it out.* She dialed the number Cade had given her, but getting only his answering machine, she hung up after giving him a very brief version of what Horne had said. She continued to worry at the situation and finally called the sheriff's office, asking for Paul Warner. When he came on the line, she explained why she had called, reviewing Tiger's actions last night and Henry Horne's accusations this morning. "It may not be anything at all related, Deputy Warner," she apologized. "I couldn't reach Cade Colby, and I wanted to let someone know, just in case. . . ." her voice trailed off.

"Thank you, Ms. Gregg," the deputy said. "We're familiar with Mr. Horne. We've certainly never had cause to think his complaints have been anything than teenagers before, but we'll check this out. Thanks for calling me." With that, he hung up. Jan looked at the phone she was holding in her hand, shook her head, and hung up.

Jan's parents were the first to arrive for the picnic, with the twins chattering away a mile a minute. "Grandpa stopped at a fireworks stand and bought lots of good stuff, AnJan! I can't wait until dark!" Jan winced; she was not fond of fireworks. "And Grandma and Grandpa took us out to breakfast, AnJan!" "Yeah—we had bacon and sausages and eggs and pancakes and *everything!*"

"Oh, well, I guess you won't be hungry in time for the picnic, will you?" Jan teased them. "So much the better— more hamburgers for the rest of us!"

"No way!" replied Trey. "I'll be ready to eat at least a dozen!"

Jan and her parents laughed. Mary Gregg said, "That might not leave enough for the rest of us, dear. Maybe you should plan on just a couple and have plenty of potato salad and other goodies. Not to mention you assured me you wanted to save room for cake!''

Jan and her mother worked together companionably in the kitchen while her father started working to get a good bed of coals going in the barbecue grill for the meat. "Did you have a nice time last night, dear?" her mother inquired.

"Oh, yes—the Mariners won, you know, in the bottom of the ninth."

"Yes, your father mentioned they'd won. Was there a big crowd?"

"Almost a sellout. Since it was the Bluejays, lots of Canadians came down for the game, as usual."

"I guess you must have gotten home pretty late then?"

Jan looked at her mother with fond exasperation. "Nothing happened, Mom! Cade went on home like a good boy!" She carefully said nothing about what had happened or about his offer to stay—for chivalrous reasons, of course.

"Oh, I'm sure he did, Jan," her mother said innocently. "Was I being nosy?"

"No, you were being a mother!"

"Do you like him very much, dear?"

"Yes. I like him . . . quite a lot, as a matter of fact."

Her mother shot a sharp glance at her, then looked down at the tossed salad she was preparing. "He seems like a nice young man. What does he do?"

"Um . . . he works for the government, I think. He's on vacation right now. And he, uh, likes fishing! As a matter of fact," she added mischievously, "the first time we met him he gave us a salmon!" She laughed. "You should have seen what it looked like after I tried to clean it!" They both laughed.

The phone rang then. It was Phyllis to complain that

they'd just missed the ferry and would have to wait half an hour for the next one.

"No problem, Phyll. We're flexible!"

Cheryl and David Norris walked the short distance between their houses instead of driving, Emily and Robby racing on ahead of them. David carried a great big bowl of potato salad, and Cheryl carried a large jar of pickled carrots she had prepared herself. "My specialty!" she explained.

An hour later Phyllis and Roy arrived, and introductions were made. As was often the case, the women gathered in the kitchen, the men around the barbecue, and the kids were back and forth between them, as well as running around the yard. Jan had planned their meal for about one o'clock, and as the hour grew closer, she worried that Cade might not make it. Who knew what might have come up?

However, just as they had everything out on the table, and John Gregg was telling everyone to "Come and get one of my world-famous hamburgers!", Cade drove into the driveway.

Jan walked around to greet him. "Is everything okay?" she asked worriedly.

Cade took the chance to pull her close and kiss her. "Shouldn't it be?" he temporized.

"Did you get my phone call?" Jan asked, and when he nodded, she added, "What do you think?"

Trey and Robby came roaring around the corner of the house, chasing Tiger, who had grabbed a dropped hot dog. They were diverted at the sight of Cade having arrived and rushed over to greet him. Cade looked at Jan over their heads and smiled with a helpless shrug, and mouthed, "Later." She smiled at him as they went into the backyard.

Greetings and introductions, where needed, ensued. Cade

apologized for being late, and everyone dug into the gargantuan meal. Lighthearted conversation and laughter filled the air, with everyone agreeing that John Gregg's hamburgers were indeed the best, at least in the west. The leftovers, of which there were many, were popped in the refrigerator, to come out again for supper.

After allowing a comfortable period of digestion, the children teased the adults into a softball game out in the south field between the Norris and Trehearne properties. After Tiger ran off with the ball for the third time, Mary Gregg insisted he sit beside her and watch. From time to time a passing car would honk, its passengers giving friendly waves.

When Tiger escaped from Mrs. Gregg and ran off with the ball, all the children gave chase, and the adults agreed it was a good time to pause for refreshment. Soon they were collapsed comfortably in the lawn chairs, each with his or her favorite cool drink, while the kids continued to chase Tiger, who thought it great fun.

By six o'clock, everyone agreed they could eat again, and out came the food for a reprise. While they worked, Phyllis whispered to Jan, "I *like* him!"

"Who? Roy?"

"No, silly, your Cade."

"You mean you don't like Roy?"

"Yes, I like him! I mean *really, really* like him! Maybe even," she said dreamily, "love him."

Jan smiled at her friend. "Got it bad, hmm?"

Phyllis nodded, "Yup. But I was saying—I like Cade. And I can tell you do, too!"

Jan smiled again, dreamily. "Oh, yes." Then she said abruptly, "Does it show that much?"

"Well, of course I know you pretty well, so I can tell. And your mom obviously can see it!"

"Yes, she was giving me the third degree earlier."

The food was enjoyed just as much the second time around, with an emphasis this time on hot dogs. Tiger was alert for any dropped or tossed bits of food. "Better than a garbage disposal," John Gregg declared. They all dawdled over the cake and watermelon, Robby and Trey having a watermelon seed spitting contest. Soon the men, too, were participating, egged on by jeers and teasing.

Jan looked around at her family and friends, replete and happy. Her eyes caught Cade's, and she could feel the electricity spark between them. His eyes promised wonderful delights, and hers responded in kind.

John Gregg watched the exchange but said nothing. However, after the modest fireworks were over and most of the other company had left, he gave a big yawn and asked Jan if she'd mind if he and Mary stayed overnight since it was so late. Jan and Cade exchanged a disappointed look, but she told her father that would be fine. "You can have Char and Tom's room, Dad."

"Come on, Grandpa and Grandma, you can read to us before we go to bed—just like last night," and they carried off their grandparents upstairs, unconsciously giving Cade and Jan a little time alone.

"Sorry about that," Jan said regretfully to Cade.

He laughed ruefully. "I think your father doesn't trust me," he teased her. "And he's right!" he murmured as he pulled her into his arms. Holding her close, his lips met hers unerringly in a long, passionate kiss. When they finally came up for air, she was clutching his shoulders for stability. "Wow!" she said. "Maybe it *is* just as well they're staying overnight!'' She reached up and pulled his head down to hers again.

He kissed her twice lightly, then wrapped his arms around her even more tightly, scattering a series of light kisses on her forehead, eyelids, cheeks, and chin before again pressing his mouth to hers in a devastating kiss that had them both seeing stars and fireworks again.

Well, it is *the Fourth of July,* she thought dazedly, her heart thundering in time with his.

He lifted his mouth from hers. His eyes were burning, and his body unmistakably wanted hers. He held her close for a few more minutes, then sighed. ''I'm sorry, honey— didn't mean to get so carried away.'' He smiled at her crookedly.

Tremulously she smiled back. ''I think that was pretty mutual.''

''Yeah, well . . . I guess I'd better be going.'' He kissed her again lightly. ''Walk me to my car?''

They went out the front door, his arm around her shoulders, her arm around his waist. ''This was a great day, honey,'' Cade said as they went down the walk to the car.

''Yes, it was, wasn't it? I'm so glad you were able to be here with us. Everyone liked you!''

''I'm not so sure about your dad,'' Cade retorted wryly.

''Oh, yes, he likes you. It's just that he can't stop being a father watching over his little girl.''

''Well, he's certainly got some little girl!''

''Why, thank you, sir, for those kind words!'' Jan said in her primmest voice, twinkling up at him.

He chuckled as he hugged her close, then moved his hands to cup her face, leaned over and kissed her gently on her lips before getting in the Bronco. ''Good night, sweetheart. Have a good night's sleep,'' he said in his deep, smoky voice.

''Thanks, Cade. You, too.''

Yeah, sure, he thought as he backed out of the driveway.

And as he drove away, Jan thought, *Oh, rats, I forgot to ask him if anyone talked to old Henry Horne.*

The next few days were surprisingly tranquil. Jan's parents left mid-morning on Monday. The breakfast conversation had reprised the picnic and those present. Jan could tell that her parents had liked Cade—actually, they both told her so. Her dad made a few fatherly remarks, and her mother's sharp eyes saw more than Jan was yet able to admit, even to herself, but Mary didn't push. Her parents were also very pleased that Char, Tom, and the twins had such nice neighbors in the Norris family, even though Char and Tom had not yet had the opportunity to get acquainted with them.

After their grandparents left, Trey and Tallie scuffed around the yard, in and out of the house, complaining that there was nothing to do. Jan had several succinct suggestions, including cleaning their rooms and working in the garden. They suddenly found ways to keep busy away from Jan, hoping for out of sight, out of mind, Jan deduced. Tiger was quiet, sleeping a lot. Evidentally all the company and excitement had worn him out, too. Lunch was picnic leftovers; dinner was disguised leftovers.

Tuesday turned drizzly, and Jan reminded the twins there were still many boxes not unpacked since the move. She targeted the upstairs linen closet for emptying, cleaning, and refilling from several of the boxes that were marked BATHROOM LINENS and BEDROOM LINENS. Such an old house had high ceilings, and Jan sent Trey to get the five-foot wooden ladder in order to clear, then clean, the top two shelves. The second-from-the-top shelf had some old crocheted dresser scarfs and antimacassars, which caused Jan to exclaim at the fine handwork contained in them. While Jan was examining them, Trey reached up to the top shelf and found some old games and puzzles. He handed them down to Tallie before coming down the ladder to look at them too. There was an old game of Monopoly, some checkers, pickup sticks, a bag of marbles, an old road-racing game from the mid 1920s, and a deck of Old Maid cards.

There were also three puzzles, the edges of the boxes raggedy. One of the puzzles was of downtown Seattle in 1937, which meant the tallest building was the old Smith Tower, dwarfed today by the many skyscrapers built in the 1980s. The children regarded the puzzles and games as a precious treasure trove and made off with them in delight, conveniently forgetting they were supposed to be helping Jan.

She opened her mouth to call them back, then shrugged. She'd probably make better progress without them and not have to listen to them grumble. Perhaps not the best train-ing, but Char and Tom could worry about that! Finishing the linen closet in time for a late lunch, Jan saw that the morning's drizzle had not stopped. Quickly preparing some sandwiches, she called the children down. They were still exuberant about the new games, even though they already had some of the same ones. But there was something about such an unexpected find plus the fact that other children, long before them, had played with these games, that caught Tallie and Trey's imaginations. During lunch, they specu-lated on those earlier children.

They teased Jan into playing some of the games after

lunch. They spent a spirited hour on Old Maid, then moved on to the pickup sticks, none of them able to pick them all up without penalty. Then they tried piecing together one of the puzzles, a spooky old mansion surrounded by ghostly, moss-draped trees. By mid-afternoon the drizzle had ceased, and by mutual agreement they decided to take Tiger and go to the beach.

"Maybe we'll see Cade!" Trey suggested.

"Do you suppose he's fishin' again?" Tallie asked.

But they saw no sign of Cade, and it wasn't just the twins who were disappointed. Tiger enjoyed the romp, however, and they all appreciated the fresh air, damp though it was, after spending much of the day indoors. Jan led the twins in a discussion of all they'd seen and done since they'd moved to Whidbey Island, including the new friends they'd made. And, of course, the new member of the family, Tiger. Mom and Dad were sure going to be surprised and happy when they got home, weren't they?

Tuesday it didn't rain, but it was overcast and cool. A perfect day to pull out those rascally weeds popping up in the garden. Many of their vegetable seeds had come up, but the chickweed, dandelions, buttercups, and grass were crowding the desired veggies. Gardening was still new enough that the twins were still enthusiastic, and they all ended up splattered with mud.

"Maybe this wasn't such a great idea," Jan said as she looked at them and herself.

"Maybe we should go swimmin' in the pond," Trey suggested hopefully, as he had numerous times before.

"No, Trey. Remember, we have to know how clean or polluted that water is before we try that."

"Well, the frogs are healthy!"

"Yes, well, they're not as picky as we are. That's their

native habitat, not ours.'' Jan walked over to where the hose was attached to the spigot at the back of the house, twisted the faucet to a full "on" position, then turned quickly toward the twins, spraying them with cold water. "Ah-ha! So you want an outside bath, do you!" she yelled at them. "How about this?"

They yelled and ran away, but they put their heads together, rallied, and attacked her simultaneously, managing to get the hose away from Jan and turn the nozzle in her direction. She shrieked, and the battle was on, ended finally by her hollering "Uncle," to their great satisfaction; and they all went inside to clean up and put on dry clothes.

While they ate lunch later, Jan asked, "Anyone for the movies?" The suggestion was greeted eagerly, and Jan got out the newspapers to see what was playing where. They ended up choosing the new Muppet movie at the one of the Everett Mall cinemas, and were ready to leave shortly thereafter. Following the movie, a big hit with all of them, they stopped for a Chinese dinner, the twins having a fit of the giggles over the fortune cookie predictions.

They encountered showers off and on during the trip home, staying inside the ferry instead of going out on deck for the trip as they usually did. When they got home, not only did Tiger give them a rousing welcome, but just a little later Cade drove up, looking a little worried. "Where have you been?" he asked edgily, and the twins supplied the information with much zest.

Jan looked at him worriedly. "Has something . . . happened?"

"Well . . . no," he replied. "But you weren't here. I came by earlier a couple times . . . I was worried," he confessed.

"I'm sorry," Jan said quickly. "It didn't occur to me to leave a note—or call."

"Hey, Cade," Trey interrupted, "have you caught the bad guys yet? What's happenin'?"

"No, not yet," Cade replied, "but we're still working on it." He turned to leave. "I just wanted to . . . say hi." He didn't want to admit how worried he had been. He really *did* have it bad!

Jan smiled at him tremulously. Why, he *had* been worried, she thought giddily. Maybe he did care . . . maybe he was really interested! "Kids, go let Tiger out," she instructed, then turned to Cade. "Can you stay for a while?" she inquired hopefully.

"No, I'm afraid not," Cade responded regretfully. "Duty calls."

"Is there anything . . . we should . . . worry about?"

"No, actually, things are pretty quiet as far as we can tell, but we're trying to stay on top of things." Then he added grimly, "Three more users have died up in Vancouver. We really need to keep this China white out of the States if we can—or at least limit it as much as possible."

"Oh, Cade, how awful! Is there anything I can do?"

"Just be very careful. I don't really think they'll be back here, or I wouldn't leave you here alone." He caught her hands and pulled her closer to him. "I don't want anything to happen to you," he said gruffly, in the deep voice that always sent shivers through her, leaning over and rubbing his cheek against hers.

Her breath caught in her throat, and thoughts of heroin, addicts, and crooks fled from her mind while her body went on red alert. Their eyes met, his blue ones blazing with instant desire, her brown ones melting in response. Unfortunately, what might have ensued was canceled by the spirited approach of twins and Great Dane. Cade sighed, kissed Jan's hand, and opened the door of the Bronco.

"Hey, Cade, can't you stay a while?" "We found these wonderful games and puzzles today!" The twins trotted out their best pleading to convince him to stay. He ruffled their hair and told them again he had to leave.

"I wish I could stay longer, but I can't right now. But I did want to at least stop in and say hi," he told them, but his eyes, looking over their heads into Jan's eyes, said he'd have liked to say much more—to her.

The twins were discussing Tiger's find of the previous week and wondered what the sheriff and others were doing about the smuggling. Jan paid scant attention, as she put out fresh food and water for Tiger, that the twins' voices had lowered and their heads were close together. When she went into the living room, she found that the twins had gone on upstairs. Mildly surprised, she decided to sit down and read the paper in peace, not realizing that a new Joe Hardy and Nancy Drew were upstairs making plans to capture the criminals themselves.

Chapter Ten

The next morning, the twins were out the door immediately after breakfast. Jan, rather surprised at their hurried departure, sat back down at the table for another cup of tea. She then puttered around the house, did some laundry, talked on the phone first to Phyllis, who was happy to relate the progress of her summer romance with Roy, then to another friend from school. Later in the day, she had a call from Tiger's former owners, now in Alaska, who wanted to know how he was adjusting. She assured Mrs. Sawley that Tiger was settling in very well and they all loved him. Jan related the story of his encounter with the skunk and the necessary tomato juice bath, which left Mrs. Sawley laughing. "We miss him," she said, "but I know he's better off with you. We appreciate that you're giving him such a good home."

When she called the twins for lunch, they came in dusty and dirty. "What in the world have you two been up to?"

she asked, and got vague replies of something they were building out behind the barn.

"You kids are supposed to stay out of the barn, remember?" she ordered.

"Yeah, sure!" "Of course, AnJan!" "We're not doin' nothin' wrong!"

"No, we're buildin' a . . ." Tallie began.

"A doghouse!" Trey interjected, looking at Tallie.

"Yeah, a doghouse for Tiger!" she agreed.

Jan looked dubiously from one to the other and started to ask a further question, when the phone rang again. While she answered it, the twins took their sandwiches and drinks and escaped outdoors to avoid more questions and to finish constructing their elaborate booby trap for the "desperados," as they'd been dubbed, but Jan called them back in.

"Emily and Robby would like to have you come over this afternoon," she said, adding drolly, "They thought you might be interested in a little horseback riding." The suggestion was greeted with wild whoops of agreement, and their booby traps quickly went back "on the shelf." They quickly finished lunch and went off across the field for an afternoon with their new friends and the horses.

However, being sidetracked for the afternoon did not cancel the enthusiasm and perseverance of Joe Hardy and Nancy Drew, who agreed that evening they should take turns watching the backyard and the barn. Tallie was nervous until Trey pointed out all they had to do was take turns watching out their bedroom windows with the binoculars. "I'll take the first watch," Trey said importantly. "I'll wake you up about midnight, and you can watch for a while."

"Can I sleep in your room, too? I don't want to be alone when I'm watchin'," Tallie requested. Each of them had a set of bunk beds that often accommodated an overnight friend.

"Sure. That'll make it easier," Trey agreed. "We don't want to wake AnJan."

"No, we don't!" Tallie responded. "Do you suppose she'll mind? We don't want her checkin' on us—or she might have me sleep with her if she thinks I'm scared."

"Wait until she goes back downstairs, Tallie, then you come on in my room, okay?"

And so it was agreed that Drew and Hardy would join forces and keep watch through the night. Among other things the intrepid pair had prepared for intruders in the barn were small piles of junk just inside each door. Hopefully any intruders wouldn't notice and would stumble over the debris. They'd debated tying ropes across about two feet off the floor but decided that would be more apt to tip off bad guys.

After Jan had kissed them good night and gone back downstairs, Tallie tiptoed into Trey's room. They were well prepared with not only the binoculars from their father's desk, but they had also arranged for a supply of cookies and chips to while away the time. Tiger kept them company and scarfed down the crumbs, considering this a wonderful way to spend the night.

Tallie finally fell asleep in the bottom bunk, and Trey settled by the window, which he had raised about two feet above the casement. After a while, chilly, he pulled a blanket off his bed and wrapped it around his shoulders to stay warm. A little later, he got his pillow and set it on the windowsill, leaning his elbows on it and looking through the binoculars from time to time. Before long, however, his eyelids got heavier, and he decided to rest his head on his arms for "just a few minutes." The next thing he knew, daylight had arrived, and Tallie was shaking him awake.

"You fell asleep!" she accused.

"Uh . . . yeah, I guess so." He was angry with himself, and his annoyance sounded in his voice. "I didn't mean to—I was just going to rest my eyes for a few minutes. . . ."

They both peered out the window but saw nothing unusual. Trey yawned. "I'm sure I would have waked up if anything had been going on," he assured his sister.

She looked at him doubtfully but didn't argue. Boys could get upset over the silliest things sometimes! She noticed Tiger standing by the door. "It looks like Tiger wants out. I'll take him downstairs and let him outside. *He'll* know if anyone's been out there!"

Trey looked ready to argue, but followed Tallie and Tiger downstairs. The twins watched carefully as Tiger went outside and made his rounds. Nothing seemed to arouse his curiosity, however, and he was soon at the back door, ready to come in and have some breakfast. They looked at each other and shrugged, then went back upstairs, agreeing, in whispers, that Tallie should go get in her own bed so AnJan wouldn't ask questions. They both went back to sleep and slept in later than usual.

Jan was surprised that the twins were so late coming down for breakfast but didn't ask questions, just enjoyed the peace and quiet and had two extra cups of tea with her novel propped up on the table in front of her.

Cade called that morning, and they had a brief, unsatisfying conversation. Both wanted to spend more time together, but circumstances were not proving convenient. Jan invited him for dinner, but that wasn't possible, so she suggested lunch. That *was* possible, and although she could have wished the twins elsewhere, so she and Cade could have the time alone together, she wasn't sure how to arrange it at such late notice. She prepared some chicken salad for sandwiches, carrot and celery sticks, fruit salad, and—what else?—chocolate chip cookies for dessert.

As he was leaving after lunch, Cade thanked her for the delicious meal and the bag of cookies she'd given him to take with him, then said, "Jan, it looks like I can get some time off Friday evening. Would you like to go out to dinner? What are the possibilities of getting a baby-sitter?"

"I'll see what I can do." Jan's eyes brightened. Wonderful—an entire evening with Cade! "I *will* find someone!" she assured him as she walked out to the car with him.

"Good!" Cade watched the twins and Tiger rambling around the yard together. "They're great kids, and Tiger's a nice mutt, but I think we're old enough to do without chaperones, don't you?"

Jan agreed, nodding. Cade tipped her head up to his, gave her a quick kiss on the nose, a longer kiss on the lips, then framed her face with his hands, looking into her eyes intently. "Jan . . ."

"Yes?" she said breathlessly.

"I . . . you're very . . . *very* special," he murmured.

She raised her hands to his chest. "And so are you," she whispered.

He kissed her again, lightly, then lifted his head as the dog and the twin terrors came racing toward them, yelling teasingly, "Cade and AnJan, sitting in a tree, K-I-S-S-I-N-G . . ."

Cade looked at Jan ruefully and shrugged his shoulders, then twirled an imaginary mustache. "Curses, foiled again!" Jan giggled at the twins' puzzled look. As Cade

drove away, Jan's mind was busy with the baby-sitting situation for Friday.

That evening Tallie "Nancy Drew" and Trey "Joe
Hardy" surreptiously made arrangements to try once again
sitting up and watching the barn and backyard for intruders.
These arrangements of course included another cache of
goodies, including some of the new batch of chocolate chip
cookies they'd all made that afternoon. They'd also gotten
the alarm clock out of their parents' room so that if one of
them fell asleep on watch it wouldn't be for long.

Jan had spent much of the afternoon assembling Tom's
computer so she could write some letters and do some les-
son plans for the coming year. Her stay on the island had
given her several ideas to use with her students. Once the
twins were tucked in, hugged, and kissed, she took her
shower and put on her pajamas and robe, then went back
downstairs to work. All the lights in the house were off
except the one over the computer, and she kept at it until
she started yawning. She stood up and stretched, noting that
it was getting on toward midnight and past time to go to
bed. She flipped off both computer and light and headed
upstairs, turning lights on and off as she progressed. Her
room faced the front of the house, and she was in bed, with
lights out, within a few minutes.

Trey was still awake in his room and heard his aunt's
progress. He carefully shone the flashlight on the clock and
decided he'd wait a little while before waking Tallie. He
flicked off the flashlight and took up the binoculars again,
sweeping the yard and outbuildings carefully. Nothing. Tiger was lying near the foot of the bed, making snuffly
snorts as he slept.

Another half hour passed, and Trey yawned hugely.
About time to wake Tallie for her watch, he thought. She'd

really give him a bad time if he fell asleep again! He gave the backyard another cursory sweep with the binoculars, then stopped and looked back to his left again. Was that a movement? He swept the north side of the yard more carefully. Yes! A movement—and a small flash of light. Could it be the smugglers? Trey watched for another minute or two, then quiety shook Tallie.

"Tallie, Tallie," he whispered, shaking her shoulder. "Wake up! I think someone's in the backyard!"

Tallie woke quickly. "What . . ."

"Shh! Be quiet! I think someone's out in the backyard!"

Tallie's eyes opened wide in alarm. "Wh-what are we going to do? I know—we can call 911!"

"No, silly, we're going to catch them ourselves!" bragged Trey in a hushed voice, puffing up his chest. "Come on, get some clothes on!" He was busy putting on jeans and shirt over his pajamas, then pulling on his socks and shoes.

Tallie sat up and swung her legs to the floor. "I don't know, Trey, I'm kind of scared! Let me look."

She went to the window and picked up the binoculars, peering into the backyard. "Where are they?" she whispered.

Trey looked over her shoulder. "There! See that flicker of light? Looks like they're heading for the barn, Tallie. Come on!" he said impatiently. "Let's get out there."

"Trey—I don't think this is a good idea. Let's call AnJan," she pleaded, still whispering.

"What happened to Nancy Drew?" Trey asked scornfully.

Against her better judgment and fears, Tallie emulated Trey by putting on her jeans and shirt over her pajamas and slipping her feet into her shoes. "What are we going to do, Trey?'' she whispered. ''Those are grownups—bigger than us. *Mean* men!''

''We're going to spy on them and see what they're doing; then we'll call Cade.'' He picked up the flashlight and beckoned her. ''Come on, Tallie, follow me.''

Tiger, awake and curious, followed them as they tiptoed down the stairs to the back door and opened it a crack. Quiet. They slipped carefully through the door, forcing Tiger to stay inside. Then they heard the creak of the barn door as someone pulled it open, then a thud and a muffled curse. Their eyes met in mutual congratulation. Their booby trap had worked!

Back in the house, Tiger sat by the door, head tipped to one side, waiting for the twins to come back in. He gave a soft woof of impatience.

By the time the twins, dodging and bending low, reached a place where they could peer through the cracks between the boards on the side of the barn, they could hear the low voices of at least two people. Tallie tugged at Trey's arm and gestured toward the house with her head. ''Come *on,* Trey,'' she whispered. ''Let's go call AnJan and let her know someone's out here!''

Not only did Nancy Drew have cold feet, but Joe Hardy's feet were chilling down as well. Trey nodded, and as they turned to go back to the house, someone grabbed them from behind. Both kids yelled, screamed, kicked, and hit out with their arms. The two men inside the barn came tumbling out to see what was wrong, but by the time they helped their partner in crime muffle the twins' cries, Tiger, still inside, had gone instantly into his loudest barking, scratching at the back door and carrying on enough to wake the dead.

Jan, going from a deep sleep into instant alarm, leaped

from her bed and turned on the light, then raced downstairs. "What is it, Tiger?" she asked, then opened the back door for him, turning on the outside light at the same time. Tiger went roaring toward the barn, and Jan could see some figures there. The hand over Tallie's mouth slipped, and she screamed as loudly as she could, "*Help!*"

Without thought, Jan went racing through the yard, hard on Tiger's heels, but before she reached the struggling figures, Tiger was leaping at first this man, then that, growling and barking and generally raising havoc.

"Trey! Tallie!" Jan screamed. "Where are you? What's happened?" She didn't notice the pain in her feet as she raced across the rough yard, over rocks and nettles. She was too intent on reaching and saving the children. As she got there, she started pulling the hair of the man holding Tallie, beating on his shoulder and arm that held Tallie so tightly. This forced him to drop Tallie to turn on Jan. Then Tiger was there, lunging at the man with teeth bared, growling and trying to bite him.

"Tallie, run for the house! Call 911—call Cade! *Hurry!*" she yelled, heading for the man holding Trey, yanking at the man's arm, kicking at his shins, sending sharp pain through her toes. Ignoring the pain, she then jabbed her fingers toward his eyes, screaming at him to let Trey go. Trey joined in, biting the man's hand and getting a good kick in on one of the man's knees. The man grunted and dropped Trey, but grabbed hold of Jan.

"Trey! Run! Go get help! Quick! Call Cade! Call 911! *Go—now!*" As she shouted this, she lifted her knee quickly, trying to knee the man in the groin, but he twisted aside, then grabbed her by the hair and twisted her arm behind her back. Jan continued to scream and kick until the pain in her arm and shoulder became too great. The man moved his hand from her hair to her mouth, to stop her screaming.

Tiger again came to her assistance, closing his teeth around the man's back pocket and part of his behind. A tearing sound came from the pants fabric, and a howling from the man, who released Jan's arm to swing his doubled-up fist back at the dog. The man's movement loosened his grip on her mouth, and she bit down on his fingers, and he gave another yell and pulled that hand away. However, the third man closed in on her, swinging a fist at her that, had it landed, would probably have broken her jaw or given her a concussion. Fortunately she ducked, and the fist instead hit her previous captor, who fell to the ground, then got groggily to his hands and knees before staggering to his feet again.

In the distance, she could hear sirens and yelling, and one of the intruders cursed and yelled, "It's the cops! Let's get outta here!"

"We can't leave all this stuff here!" another one said.

"Forget it!"

"Let's grab the chick and take her with us—they won't dare shoot then."

Grunting, the third man grabbed Jan's arm roughly and started dragging her after him. She hit at him with her other fist, trying to dig in her heels. Tiger badgered him from the other side.

"Get rid of that dog, Bud!" her captor ordered.

Jan saw the glint of a gun as the man tried to point it at Tiger. "*No!*" she screamed, and renewed her efforts to free herself. "Don't shoot him!"

"Then you better stop fightin', lady, or you're both dead meat!"

They were dragging her north through the pasture and

toward Henry Horne's woods. Tiger was still darting in and out, and Jan kept trying to drag her feet, which by now were very painful. The man paused to throw Jan over his shoulder, then continued as fast as he could. Jan pounded on his back as she was jostled up and down, the blood running to her head, yelling at him to put her down. She could see there were flashing lights on the road and over at the house, and she could hear men's loud voices chasing after them as well as closing in from the road.

"Come out of there with your hands up," a voice of authority yelled.

"No way! We got the chick here, Smoky! You try anything, and she gets hurt!"

"Let me go!" Jan continued to struggle as her captor trotted along, jabbing his back with her elbow and kicking her feet below where he held her knees. He gave her a hard, open-handed slap on the face, and she yelped again. Tiger tried to come to the rescue by getting in front of the man, causing him to trip and fall. Jan had the presence of mind to roll clear, then scuttled away on her hands and knees as fast as she could while Tiger was snarling and barking at the downed man.

Jan paused after she'd scooted several yards, got to her knees, and carefully peered back over her shoulder to see how far she was from the men. She could hear them muttering to one another. "What do you mean, she got away? Now we got no hostage!" "It's that dog! Kill 'im!"

Without a second thought, Jan called to Tiger, thinking only to save him, not that the men would hear and follow. But she did again start crawling through the grass as fast as she could. Then she thought to call out to the police, "Hey, they don't have me anymore—go get 'em!"

But of course, it was dark, and they hesitated to shoot.

The smugglers wavered over whether to try to capture her again or run, and running won the day. They didn't get far, for as they raced through Henry Horne's woods, Horne, who had been awakened by the racket, was standing by with his shotgun and let loose a couple of rounds in their direction. The crook with the gun snapped off a couple of shots back, and then the police had spotlights trained on the woods, and some of the law enforcement officers had run around behind them, and soon the crooks found themselves encircled and came out, hands raised in the air, accusing one another for their failure.

Jan sat on the damp ground, cold and scared, and hugged Tiger, afraid to move. Back at the house, she could see more people moving around the yard, in and out of the barn. Soon she heard a hoarse whisper. "Jan! Where are you? It's Cade!"

"Oh, Cade!" she whispered back. "Is it really you? I'm over here!" He followed the sound of her voice, which was joined by Tiger's whine, and soon had his arms around her. As she threw her arms around him, she gasped out, "I'm so glad you're here!"

"Are you okay, honey?" he asked urgently.

Safe in his arms, she started crying. "Y-y-yes," she sniffed, "I th-think so." He hugged her tightly against him, both of them now sitting on the ground. "Oh, sweetheart, you're still in your nightclothes! And no shoes, either. You must be freezing. Here," he said, taking off his jacket, "let's put this around you."

Jan didn't remember a lot about getting back to the house, just that she was carried snugly in Cade's arms. The twins, crying and terrified, flung themselves at her and wouldn't let go. They all crowded into the kitchen, and the twins sobbed even louder as they saw their aunt all scratched and bruised, her clothes torn. Her feet were scratched and cut, dirty and oozing blood. Her auburn curls were standing on end, full of twigs and leaves, and her brown eyes looked like coals in her white face. The twins, mussed, torn, and bruised themselves, cried even louder, and Jan put her arms around them, holding them close; and Cade put his arms around them all, thankful to have them safe.

Daylight had long since arrived before things settled down. Once assured that the bad guys had been captured, along with a considerable amount of China white heroin, some in the barn, the rest in the pickup they'd pulled a little way into Henry Horne's woods, the twins perked up and were once again clever Nancy Drew and courageous Joe Hardy. Jan felt like fainting when they told their story and she remonstrated with them about going out there on their own. Cade scolded them for not first calling their aunt, then him or 911 for help. Tiger was petted and praised for his defense of his family.

It appeared that Johnnie Rollins was indeed involved in the drug smuggling, and it was the sight of his pickup truck in the neighborhood that had first alerted the local authorities; that and the twenty-six-foot inboard boat, the *Serena*, anchored near the boat launch earlier.

At about the same time the truck was observed, near midnight, Cade had been returning from a meeting in Seattle and had spotted the boat. A rowboat was pulled up on the beach, and he had appropriated it to approach the larger boat. When no one responded to his "Hello the *Serena*— anyone aboard?" he had gone aboard. Traces of what the boat had transported, transshipped, as it later turned out, from a Panamanian-registered freighter steaming just off the Strait, were evident to the trained eye, and he used his cell phone to alert his network. When he heard in return that Rollins's pickup truck had been spotted in the neighborhood, his inner alarm went off. The truck had not yet been located—it had disappeared in this neighborhood!

Cade recalled Henry Horne's complaint and urged that units be sent to the area, and by the time he was ashore and heading up the hill to protect Jan and the twins, chaos had broken loose. He had run as fast as he could the last five hundred yards, finding the twins in tears, shaking and terrified. Tiger could be heard out in the field barking and snarling enough to raise the dead. Simultaneously, Cade's associates had found the truck and were warning the smugglers to come out. Cade was communicating the news that Jan was their captive just as the crooks called out that news. Sternly telling the children to stay where they were, Cade had started off through the field, gun drawn, his heart in his throat, to rescue Jan. As it turned out, she had just escaped.

After they had been captured, Rollins and his partners in crime blamed one another for the fiasco, with plenty of blame going to Jan, the twins, and Tiger. His partners accused Rollins of negligence, as well as stupidity, for not telling them the property had changed hands and it was no longer safe to hide the drugs in the old barn anymore. All in all, as someone commented, "Ineptness ruled."

Jan, after a hot soak in the tub, dressed gingerly in some loose slacks and shirt. Before dressing, she viewed her body in the mirror, shuddering at the maze of bruises and scratches on her. In a few days, she would have a Technicolor body! Every step hurt, and she painfully acknowledged it would be a long time before she felt like dancing. Cade insisted on gently treating, then wrapping, her poor, abused feet.

Cheryl Norris, who, along with most of the neighbors, had been awakened by the sound and fury, had come down to help out and told Cade she'd stay there with Jan and the twins until he was able to return. She fixed them some breakfast and lots of coffee for the law enforcement officers who were still following up on the various necessary activities. Later Emily and Robby came down, and the twins, feeling very self-important, related to a rapt audience what had happened. Their activities were, of course, featured, and they took at least part of the credit for capturing the smugglers.

It was late in the afternoon before Cade was able to get back. "No—don't get up," he said to Jan, sitting down beside her. He put his arms around her on the couch, holding her close. "Jan, you'll never know how scared I was when I realized they had you! You idiot! Why didn't you call us?"

"Cade, they had the twins," she said simply. "I didn't even think—I just went running out to save them!"

"Yes, that *is* what you would do." He nuzzled her neck and held her closer.

"And who was it who risked his life to come out in that field to save me?" she teased, putting her arms around him, too, leaning against him, closing her eyes. Safety! But not just safety, she thought—love! But how could it be? They'd known each other such a short time. . . .

Cade tipped her head up so he could kiss her, gently, on the lips. "How could I not?" he inquired. Cade smiled into her soft brown eyes, the dark blue of his boldly possessive. His soft, deep voice rumbled in his chest as he asked, "I hope you're not completely turned off on islands after what's happened here on Whidbey."

"Well, no . . . no, I don't think I am. After all, it wasn't the *island's* fault!" she pointed out.

"I'm glad to hear that," Cade murmured, kissing her nose and running his hand through her vibrant hair. "But . . . how does the island of . . . Maui sound?" he inquired, trailing his lips across her cheek.

Enjoying the sensation of his lips, the soft warmth of his breath, she wasn't paying close attention to his words. The electricity between them had both hearts beating a tattoo.

"Hmm?" she breathed against his lips.

"Maui," he repeated. "How does Maui sound to you?"

"Mmm . . . wonderful," she replied. "Magical . . ."

"How does it sound for a honeymoon?" he queried softly as he nibbled on her ear.

It took a minute to sink in, and she leaned back and looked into his smiling eyes. Trembling, she asked, "Are you asking me . . ."

"Yes, sweet Jan, I'm asking you to be my wife. I love you," he added in a quiet, sincere rumble, as though in afterthought.

She threw her arms around his neck. "Yes! Yes! To marriage, and Maui—and you!"

"Just you and me, right? No twins?" he teased.

"No!"

"No dog?"

"No!"

"No skunk?" He was grinning now, his eyes twinkling.

"No!" she assured him, then excitedly jumped up and started whirling around in joy, ignoring the pain in her feet. "Just you and me!"

"Good!" he replied, standing up, grasping her around the waist and swinging her around and around before stopping and pulling her close again. "Just you and me, sweetheart—forever!"

DATE DUE

OCT 8 '96	AUG 3 1 '98		
OCT 22 '96	APR 30 '99		
	JU .28 99		
DEC 11 FEB 12 '97	SEP 2 1999		
MAR 10 '97			
APR 29 '97			